The Summer That Lasted Forever

The Summer That Lasted Forever

CATHERINE PETROSKI

Houghton Mifflin Company
Boston 1984

The author gratefully acknowledges the support
of the National Endowment of the Arts for
a Fellowship in Fiction Writing.

Library of Congress Cataloging in Publication Data

Petroski, Catherine.
The summer that lasted forever.

SUMMARY: Molly approaches her twelfth birthday
still trying to accept the death of her mother several
years before and facing the imminent sale of her beloved
pony; but she finds the inner strength to cope beautifully.
  1. Children's stories, American. [1. Mothers and
daughters—Fiction. 2. Death—Fiction. 3. Ponies—
Fiction] I. Title.
PZ7.P4472Su 1984   [Fic]   84-12930
ISBN 0-395-35388-2

Printed in the United States of America

S   10 9 8 7 6 5 4 3 2 1

For Stephen

The Summer That Lasted Forever

I

_"Molly?"

Molly could hear her daddy all right, but she wasn't going to answer.

"Molly?" Daddy called again. "Molly? Come on out here, honey. This little girl wants to try out your pony."

How could he?

And of all people to want to buy the Mare! This little *girl?* This brat! Daddy might not understand about Melissa Tyde, but Molly did. How could Daddy and teachers — all adults, it seemed like — be taken in by Melissa's golden curls and blue eyes, batting away as she talked, a mile a minute? Melissa was the most spoiled, stuck-on-herself teacher's pet at Longfellow. And *she* wanted Molly's Mare!

No, Molly would not cooperate. She'd just stay inside, in the lattice porch. Where it was safe. Where she could watch and not be watched. Melissa could inspect the Mare all she wanted. Let her look all day and all night. Let Melissa even ride her, if she had to. No matter what Daddy said, this was wrong. He had given Molly the pony, and now he wanted to take it away, or at least make her sell it. Yes, wrong, and unfair. This pony could never really be anyone else's, no matter who paid who what money or what Daddy said. The Mare was Molly's forever.

Go away, Melissa! Get lost!

Melissa Tyde ... My Less Is Tied ... Molasses Tide. The name rushes back and forth in Molly's head like waves on sand, time and time again, but each wave is slightly different. The genie of the sea appears, large, in a vapor. Molly, you have but one wish left. Pray, what is it? She must choose carefully. But of course there really is no question. Genie, let Melissa Tyde be washed away to some desert island, never to be heard from again in the civilized world. Melissa never will lay eyes on Molly's Mare again, either. Good-bye, Melissa Tyde! Bon voyage, toodle-loo, good riddance.

Molly opened her eyes and peered out through the morning-glory leaves winding in and out of the lattices.

Pretending wasn't working. Neither was wishing. Big as life, Melissa still stood there in Molly's field. Melissa and Dr. Tyde appeared to be going over the pony with a fine-toothed comb. From here it looked as though Melissa knew what she was doing, but

Melissa was an expert at anything, especially at getting her own way.

Molly's heart turned. This would be a simple matter for Melissa, making her father buy Molly's Mare. Every bit of imagining in the world wouldn't change that, and neither would every bit of wishing. Melissa Tyde was a fact.

Everyone was always saying Molly had to learn to face facts.

"Molly?" Daddy called again.

All right, Molly would face facts, but from the lattice porch. These facts made Molly nervous, like having to laugh even though nothing funny was happening. Molly's daddy and her grandpa, Melissa and her father, all stood with one foot propped up on the fence rail together, like a little chorus line. Everyone in Comfort knew Dr. Tyde, the children's doctor, with his soft southern accent and a mustache so fine it looked as though it had been drawn on with one of Grandpa's bookkeeping pens. Every kid in Comfort *definitely* knew him. "Come along now," Dr. Tyde would say with a fake chuckle, and then he'd take his shot needle or tongue depressor and lie through his teeth. "This isn't going to hurt a bit," he'd always say. It always did.

Daddy glanced at the house. Molly would be hearing about why she wasn't there too, one foot up on the fence, just like everybody else. Daddy expected her to show Melissa what a nice pony the Mare was. Molly couldn't do that. If she did, the Tydes would buy the Mare for sure. Besides, why

3

should Molly explain everything it had taken her four years to figure out to know-it-all Melissa?

Why couldn't Daddy see what a mistake it would be? Melissa would never love the Mare. Ponies are work. Ponies sometimes don't do what you want them to do. Or they do what you don't want them to. They eat, day in and day out, and someone has to feed them and keep their stalls clean. Melissa didn't seem like the kind to dirty her hands. Melissa would get someone else to clean the Mare's hooves. And what if the Mare got colic or went off her feed? Would Melissa worry? Dr. Tyde could always hire someone to look after the Mare, but that just wasn't the same thing. That wasn't the same as loving.

And horses understood things like that.

Molly stayed inside the porch, watching the four figures standing in the June sun. She didn't want any part of this.

"Molly!"

Daddy wasn't fair: he could never say Molly hadn't held up her end of things, taking care of the Mare, mostly by herself. It had nothing to do with that, and everything to do with the growing. Just because Molly had grown a little. Just because she was a little too long-legged for the Mare now. What kind of reason was that to sell the Mare, to take her away?

Worst of all, Daddy had even made her tack the Mare before Melissa arrived.

"Molly?"

Molly had to do something. What if she made

Melissa *not* like the pony? If she could get the Mare to act up, Melissa might forget about ponies and go play tennis at the Comfort Country Club.

So Molly finally answered. "I'm coming, Daddy," she said. She had to.

She wiped her tears away and pulled on her boots.

Melissa tapped the crop she brought with her against the rails of the fence. They had known each other, Molly guessed, since they were — maybe nine years old, since Mrs. Bower's third-grade class. Melissa had been Wendy in the third grade's *Peter Pan*, but Molly thought she'd have made a better Captain Hook, or Crocodile.

Melissa tossed her head impatiently, her golden curls bobbing, catching the sunlight. "*Dad*-dy," she said several times, as if to say "Let's go home." But Dr. Tyde didn't budge. His foot was still on the bottom rail of the fence.

Daddy looked again toward the house. "Don't take all day, Molly," he called. "Dr. Tyde's got to get to the hospital."

Dr. Tyde, Dr. Frankenstein. "I'm coming," Molly answered. "My boots are tight." Her feet had grown too.

Above Molly, above the lattice porch, the long branches of the old elm trees moved ever so slightly. She had to go. She couldn't stay here forever. Molly asked herself: What if Mama were here? What would she say to do about this state of affairs?

If only Molly could talk to her, for just a minute.

5

Now Molly, you march yourself right out there. Running away never solved anything. Hiding on the porch isn't going to keep Melissa from buying the Mare. If she's made up her mind, that is. You don't even know that.

Molly hears the low, calm voice. It is inside her head. She looks around the lattice porch, the chairs, the glider, the big plants out for the summer. Molly could swear Mama was here. So many times Molly and Mama had sat here together to settle things, figure things out together. So many times, except once. The last time. No, the voice isn't real, and it isn't a ghost, because Molly doesn't believe in ghosts. She believes in Mama.

Molly, you're just making yourself look strange. Come on now.

Mama's voice again, gentle, encouraging. Molly hears it clearly. Mama's voice is the one thing that Molly can count on.

Let's go, Molly.

Melissa turned when she heard Molly open the screen door. With an odd little smile, Melissa watched Molly's every step as she came down the drive from the house.

Molly hadn't seen anyone so perfectly turned out since the last horse show: Melissa wore brand-new canary-colored breeches, a silky-looking sleeveless shirt with a stock tie, a beautiful pair of new black leather boots and a perfectly jet black velvet hard hat. Melissa's beautiful straw-colored curls were pulled back with a pale blue ribbon that matched her shirt. Molly noticed that Melissa had slipped up on one detail. She had put the hat's elastic under her chin. Only babies and beginners did that.

Melissa's chin jutted at its usual angle, forward and up, and except for one thing she stood motionless. Petite Melissa tapped her crop impatiently against the top of her boot.

Molly felt sick about the whole thing, but the Mare wasn't bothering to look at Melissa. Of course she didn't need to. Everybody knew horses could see things without looking straight at them. That was why horses would shy sometimes when you didn't expect it.

And why should the Mare look at Melissa? So what if this bratty kid had a crop? The Mare wasn't used to such things. Molly never used a crop. Melissa had better watch it.

"Well, Miss Molly, how you doin', darlin'?" Dr. Tyde said. This man was enough to make anyone sick who wasn't, Molly thought. Somehow, though, he had all the parents in Comfort fooled. They all thought Dr. Tyde was such a wonderful man, so kind, so concerned. Dr. Jekyll and Mr. Hyde.

Despite his charming manner, Dr. Tyde was growing impatient, maybe even a little angry. He wasn't used to being kept waiting.

Dr. Tyde smiled, his fine, wicked mustache straightening into a flat line. "That's a right nice piece of horseflesh," he said.

What an awful, creepy way of putting it, Molly

7

thought. She had to be polite, though. "Thank you, Dr. Tyde," she said. "Do you ride, too?"

"Yes, indeed, young lady. Lissy here doesn't like to hear her old daddy brag, but I was the youngest rider blooded in the Helmhill Hunt. You ever hear of the Helmhill Hunt?"

"No sir. I don't really hunt."

"No matter," Dr. Tyde said while Melissa just watched, "this pony of yours sure has won a passel of ribbons, Molly. Lissy here might like a little of the glory, too!"

Melissa beamed. "What's your pony's name, Molly?" she asked.

"It's really Morgan's Daydream, but that's too long. I just call her the Mare. That's her name now."

"Oh? How odd," Melissa said.

Molly forced herself to smile. "Have you done much riding, Melissa?"

"Oh sure," she said, "here and there." She waved her hand, and Molly smelled toilet water. She saw Melissa's fingernails with the pale pink polish. Melissa pulled on Dr. Tyde's sleeve and whispered something to him. She would. How rude, whispering in front of other people. If Molly did that, people would cluck and say, *Poor thing, no mama to teach her better.*

"Come on, Molly, Dr. Tyde can't wait all day," Daddy said. "Take her around."

When Molly put her left foot in the stirrup, she nudged the Mare, who started off before Molly got completely on. As soon as Molly got her legs down, she squeezed the Mare with all her might. The pony took off like a house afire, galloping madly around the pasture. This was the fastest she'd moved in the last two weeks. Maybe it *would* work! Molly leaned and grimaced. Anything to make it look as though the Mare was completely out of control. Finally, with an exaggerated tugging on the reins, Molly hauled the lathered pony to a halt near the Tydes. Molly noticed no feet rested on the bottom rail now.

Daddy looked suspicious. Grandpa looked puzzled. Melissa was trying to look bored. Dr. Tyde looked a little concerned, but his smile was concrete.

"Think that's got most of the pepper out of her, Melissa. She can be a handful," Molly said as sweetly as she could. "Would you like to take her around the pasture?"

Dr. Tyde cleared his throat. "I assume this animal hasn't been ridden much lately, McAfee, otherwise, I don't see how she ever won a thing. Actually, I'm late at the hospital. You under-stand —"

Melissa butted right in.

"Don't be silly, Daddy," she said sharply. "This fat old pony's not going to scare me off."

Melissa snapped the crop against her boot top, and the Mare turned her head quickly to the noise.

"You're sure?" Molly said. "She hasn't had much exercise lately. She might be a little feisty." Molly wasn't really sure how much pep the Mare had left after all that exertion. She might just poke around along the fence.

"I think another day would be better, Lissy, dar-lin'," Dr. Tyde said.

"I know what I'm doing, Daddy," Melissa said. "I came here to ride this pony, and I'm going to. They can just wait at the hospital for five more minutes." Melissa stuck the crop in her boot and crawled through the white crossbars of the fence. Molly put the reins back over the Mare's head and held them for Melissa at the saddle pommel.

"She's all yours," Molly said, hoping it wasn't true.

Accidentally Melissa stuck her left foot too far into the iron, and her toe jabbed the Mare. It was the second time today, and once was too much for the Mare. Next Melissa jumped up too hard, hit the Mare's rump when she swung her leg over, and plunked herself down heavily on the Mare's back.

Melissa wasn't doing anything right, but it was perfect! All the Mare needed was somebody crash-ing down on her back like that — she detested that.

The Mare laid back her ears. No, not the stub-born act. Molly's plan might not work after all. Me-lissa wouldn't even get the pony to move if she decided to play mule. The Mare had done this a million times, usually with Luke, Molly's cousin.

"What's *wrong* with this stupid animal?" Melissa said. "Why won't he go?"

"She," Molly corrected.

"He, she — what's the difference?" Melissa breathed short angry breaths, getting madder by the minute. Then she remembered the crop stuck in her boot. She pulled it out and cracked it loudly across the Mare's flank.

The Mare didn't move a muscle.

"Lissy, darlin', you'd better watch out there," Dr. Tyde said.

"That pony doesn't take well to crops," Daddy said, with alarm in his voice.

But Melissa wasn't listening to anybody. "I'm going to get this dumb pony to move, one way or the other." Again she cracked the Mare with the crop, one side and then the other.

"Put away the crop, Lissy," Dr. Tyde said.

"Young lady, that's no way to ride a horse, and it's certainly no way for a lady to treat an animal." Grandpa's face had turned a bright angry pink.

The Mare had her feet dug in halfway to China.

"Oh, who cares? Why should I want a dumb pony that runs like a fool one minute and won't move the next?"

"Melissa Tyde, you get down off there this minute," Dr. Tyde said.

But now the Mare had had enough. Enough of the crop. Enough of the loud talk and somebody plopping down like a sack of potatoes on her back. Without warning, she took off at a fast canter. To everyone's surprise — Melissa's, too, judging from her expression — Melissa stayed with her, at least until the Mare began to feel the crop flipping up and down on her shoulder. Molly could see that it was an accident — Melissa wasn't meaning to tap her — but the Mare started bucking. Melissa's heels weren't down, and her shoulders were back and flopping around.

So no one was surprised that in the pasture corner, at the low spot where the dewy grass grew lush and tall in the damp ground, the Mare dumped Melissa. The Mare had picked the spot.

"Oh, I'm sorry — I'm sorry," Molly said. She didn't want Melissa to get hurt, just discouraged. Dr. Tyde had ducked into the pasture and was running toward his daughter, who was thrashing the grass with her crop.

Nothing was any the worse for the fall except Melissa's new canary breeches, which obviously would have to go to the dry cleaner's. And Melissa's pride.

Daddy turned to Molly. "Why did you do that?" he demanded. His eyes were angry, and he held his mouth still now, in a straight line.

"She's OK, Daddy. Melissa's not hurt. The grass is soft."

Grandpa turned to go to the house. But he turned around again. "I know why you did that, Molly, but you haven't solved the problem. You've only made it worse."

Dr. Tyde made Melissa stand up. "Stop that thrashing, baby," he said, "and take a few steps." She did. "Nothing wrong with you," the doctor said. "Takes more than that to stop a Tyde."

He sent Melissa to their car. "I'm going to have to give this some thought, Jack," he said to Daddy, shaking hands. Molly couldn't imagine why Dr. Tyde wasn't furious. "There's not a horse we

Tydes can't ride, Mr. McAfee," he said to Grandpa. "Melissa just hasn't got a good seat yet. She'll come along . . . she'll do me proud eventually."

"This particular pony might not be such a good idea," Grandpa said.

"Nonsense. I'll give you a call, Jack," Dr. Tyde said, and left.

Molly drew in a breath for courage. "Daddy," she said, "you know the Mare is supposed to be mine. You gave her to me, remember? It's not right to take her away from me."

"You know that's not the point, Molly. We've been through this a hundred times at least. You're too big. The Mare was fine a couple of years ago, even last year. But you have to move on to other things."

"It's not fair, Daddy. She's like a person, she has feelings. And you want to take her away. Why can't I keep *something?*"

"Now you just take that pony of yours and put her away. This minute!" Daddy said. His jaw was set. Anger was cracking in his eyes. "I've seen and heard enough of you for one morning."

The Mare stood, docile as a lamb, with reins drooping into the tall grass. Sad looking. Almost sorry about what had happened. Molly picked up the reins to lead her back to the stable.

"Easy, Jack . . . easy," Grandpa said gently.

"She did that on purpose," Daddy said.

"Yes, and she thought she had reason to. Jack, I've told you before. I'm worried — really worried — about Molly."

"That makes two of us," Daddy said.

But Molly walked faster, her legs and the Mare's tearing through the tall, green, silky grass. Faster, so she couldn't hear any more of what they said.

2

Molly's lattice porch opened off the dining room, which no one used. The porch was a place of magic, where things were safe and unchanging and hushed. It was a certain, still place in a world where nothing seemed to stand still, a beautiful place, where sunshine diced the fresh cool mornings with diamonds of light and great shady afternoons seemed to last whole lifetimes. The porch had been a special place as long as Molly could remember, back to when Mama was with her here — that was the first Molly could remember of the porch. That was when the porch became special.

It was on the porch that Mama had taught Molly the Trick of Magic Seeing — controlling the amount of world you let into your eyes by moving toward or away from the white diamond lathes that made the lattices. Even then Molly knew there was no real magic to it, but Mama *called* it magic, and because they pretended so hard and so well, it seemed it was.

Now Molly tried the trick, fitting her eyes to the holes — one eye to a hole. For a moment she could forget that she was inside the porch. And then she stepped back so far she could feel the cool red bricks of the house through the back of her shirt, and she saw lattices, lattices, lattices, blotting out everything else in the world. This clean white diamond room was Molly's haven; Grandpa's magenta morning-glory, on its way to the sky, peeked its curly tendrils in to see if she was there.

Yes, she was.

Molly's imagination sometimes did funny things. Sometimes it seemed that the porch and the dining room were like people patiently waiting, listening for the explanation to finally arrive. Someday some-one would knock on the door, say "Hello, I have news for you," and come in and explain once and for all about Mama's wreck. Someone would tell why. Someone would let Mama come back for just a minute, so she and Molly could talk together one last time.

Though the accident had happened five years ago, no one was really quite used to the idea that Mama was gone. Everyone had always had such a good time at Mama's dinners, but now Grandpa and Daddy wouldn't eat in the dining room. Mama's cleaning lady, Graham, came every day now. She still kept Mama's silver polished — the coffee ser-vice, the big oval platters, the punch bowl that Mama used to fill with hot spicy punch for holiday parties. She *had* to do it, Graham said, even if nobody used them now. It was a question of morale.

"Nothing gloomier than old black silver!" Graham said with a smile. "Let things go too far," she said with her sly look, "and before you know, they're never the same again." Graham still spoke like a Southerner. She came from the Carolina mountains — "Little Scotland," she'd say. Not North or South Carolina, Graham explained; there was only *one* Carolina. "And I feel right at home with a family named McAfee."

Graham liked to sing Molly old Scots songs, or songs "just from the hills," as she shined away at Mama's silver or the wide hardwood floors in the halls. When she thought no one was looking, Graham might dance a little fling with the carpet sweeper and then turn prim and serious. When Molly was just a little girl, she used to hitch rides on Graham's carpet sweeper, with its loud, warm pillow-lung.

Molly remembered that.

Molly remembered many things.

Any past day could be real here on the lattice porch. Any day could come back in this magic place of sun and shade and dreams and memory. Anything was possible.

Mickey Mouse's white gloves were pointed to the ten and the twelve. Only ten o'clock.

The Tydes had come and gone. Molly drew up close to the lattice and looked far down in the field where the Mare grazed, lazily snipping off a few bites of grass here, a few there, getting fatter by the minute. "Ponies run to pure fat," Daddy told her. "You have to work them." As long as Molly schooled the Mare for shows, the pony was what Grandpa called "pleasingly plump." But now anybody could see that the Mare had become downright fat. And lazy, too. Rather than jump a fence, these days she'd just give it a good looking over.

This stupid growing!

These dumb long legs! Molly did want to grow up, but gradually. It was bound to happen; Molly couldn't have done anything about it any more than the Mare could do something about being a runty little Welsh pony, hardly twelve hands. The McAfees were long-legged people.

When the Mare arrived at Molly's seventh birthday party, the pony was seven years old too. They were just right for each other. At first Grandpa would give Molly a leg-up, but he didn't have to do that for long. It was the birthday after Mama died. Grandpa and Daddy had a secret brewing, but Molly never once guessed it would be a pony. It wasn't so much that the pony was to take Mama's place, but to occupy Molly's time and keep her from thinking too much about what had happened.

And Molly couldn't really talk to Daddy about it. Sometimes she would find him upstairs, his eyes red and wet.

Now Molly pushed open the lattice door. She went out, thinking, June, June, June, a summer has so many days! It looked endless and empty, especially since Daddy had made up his mind to sell the

Mare. Molly couldn't argue with what he said: she was just too big to ride the pony. But sell the pony to Melissa? Molly couldn't let that happen.

June, June, June, one, two, three, four, five, down the smooth concrete stairs, gray and still cool from the night. Molly set her mind to work.

The herringboned brick walk lay in the elms' shade. Bulges of soft moss grew between the cool, damp red rectangles. Gigantic old elm trees arched their long branches overhead, sweeping the sky.

At the end of the garden stood the arched white rose arbor that Grandpa had built just before Molly was born. Each June, at the start of every summer Molly could remember, the arbor filled with pink climbers and deep green leaves, with perfume and the hum of bees. Inside the arbor was a pair of seats where she and Mama had pretend-tea in tiny cups, with rows of polite dolls all around.

Molly tilted her head back and looked up through the very top. How could Melissa possibly want the Mare now? Anyone else would be embarrassed to death, but Melissa might be different. Melissa had said, "I'll be back." She might insist on having the Mare, just for meanness — how could Molly outthink somebody like that? Molly didn't understand the first thing about the way Melissa ticked.

"Think for yourself," Mama said.

Noon. The brewery's whistle brought Molly back from her thoughts. "Whistling girls and cackling hens," Graham maintained, "always come to no good ends." Molly whistled for the Mare anyway.

She looked up, then put her head back to the grass and took another nibble. Her head still down, the pony started toward Molly. Molly whistled again. The Mare couldn't have it appear she was eager to get to Molly. It was part of their game.

"Hi, Mare-baby."

The Mare made a low nicker. Hello between old friends.

Molly pressed her hand to the Mare's velvet nose. "Have you recovered from your morning gallop?" she asked. Long whisker sprouts tickled Molly's hand as the pony's lips played with her fingers. "You fat old thing! You surprised me, taking off like that!"

The Mare tossed her head up.

Molly was sure the Mare understood what she said. It wasn't such a far-fetched idea: the mules in the McAfee coal mines all worked by voice commands. Grandpa always said it was as much how you said things as the words themselves, but Molly wasn't so sure. Yes, the Mare could understand Molly perfectly.

"More news, sugar lump," Molly said. "Your next-most-favorite rider in the world — after Melissa — will be here this afternoon." Aunt Lizzie was coming by right after lunch, and Luke was coming with her. Molly giggled at the thought of Luke. The Mare's lips parted. Was she smiling?

"Poor old Luke!" Molly said. Melissa had brought her crop on purpose. Luke was simply inept. Unintentionally the worst rider in the world. Luke tried. He just didn't have the right touch. He might be a wonderful baseball pitcher, but he was a terrible rider.

Molly pulled a clump of timothy from outside the fence rails. "Here, Mare," she said, and the pony took the green bouquet and chewed it, studying Molly's face with her round brown eyes.

"Melissa deserved everything she got this morning. But you really should be nicer to Luke, Mare. He's my favorite cousin." The pony was too full of spring, Daddy had said, and he had punished the Mare for throwing Luke. Now Molly patted the Mare's neck. "You mustn't hold it against Luke. He didn't *mean* to hurt your mouth."

Molly crawled through the fence, all legs. She hugged the pony's neck, then swung her right leg up and over, hopping onto the pony's back as easily as breathing. The Mare began to walk, then to trot. Molly straightened up on the pony's back.

Daddy was right. Molly's legs hung way down. The Mare was rounder than ever. The pony gave a skip and began cantering. Gently, gently, around the edge of the pasture. Molly thought about Luke's fall, how he swore his ankle was broken, and even though the X-rays found nothing wrong, Luke still walked with a limp when he remembered. When Daddy took the strap to the Mare, Molly ran inside, not to see. "Don't you understand, Molly? You can't let a pony get away with that," he said sadly, "or they get dangerous."

Now slow and steady, around the fence, the Mare cantered. Molly closed her eyes, her head resting on the pony's neck.

Did horses dream? What kind of a dream did the Mare have last night?

There is no pasture, no fence. It is just a large open field, a part of the land that goes with the house. There are other houses nearby, ones that belong to Grandpa's cousins and to his brother. All of the houses, together, are known as McAfee's Addition to the Town of Comfort, State of Illinois.

Grandpa tells stories of how his *grandpa came and settled and cleared, long before Comfort was called Comfort. Just a crossroads, he says, more than a hundred years ago. Times were hard, he mentions, as if to tell Molly that other people, long ago, had their problems too and survived them all right. Wild animals and hard winters, and angry Indians and the wars over trading posts — they had a rough life. Molly can survive, too, he says with other words.*

Now Molly sees her birthday. She is seven today, and today the Mare comes to be hers. September 1. The Mare arrives in the back of Daddy's stake-sided pickup truck that reads MCAFEE COAL COMPANY *on the door. The Mare walks off onto the backyard embankment as though she has done it every day of her life.*

"That's what I call a nice calm animal," Grandpa says.

Molly can't believe the pony is hers.

The Mare waits quietly under the old elms. The whole birthday party disputes who will get to ride first. Molly decides she will ride last. She wants to look and figure out this animal, this present. The Mare looks big to her. Maybe she won't be able to make it do what she wants it to. The party rides around and around the field until the sun goes out, and after dark, after everyone else is gone, Molly rides again one last time.

"Molly," a voice called from the house. "Molly?"

"Down here, Grandpa." Molly ducked back through the Mare's fence and set out for the house at a run.

"Time to eat lunch," Grandpa said. Graham had their sandwiches and iced tea all ready. Molly had eaten all of her sweet pickle and half of her ham salad sandwich when the phone rang.

"It's for you, Molly," Grandpa said, holding the phone toward her.

"It is?"

"Yes. Your Aunt Lizzie."

"Hello, Lizzie?" Molly answered. "Oh? I don't know — I'll have to ask Grandpa."

Molly covered the phone with her hand. "Lizzie wants me to go to St. Louis. To shop for a dress. I don't need a dress, and Grandpa, when I go to St. Louis I always get sick in the car. Don't make me go, please."

"You get sick because you're always reading."

"No, I don't like to go to St. Louis."

"You need some summer clothes, don't you, Molly?"

"We can shop in Comfort. Please, don't make me

23

go all the way to St. Louis just for some old clothes."

"Molly, Lizzie's waiting. Don't be rude. She's trying to do something nice for you."

"But I like jeans and shorts. I don't need a dress."

"Molly, she's waiting."

"Will you talk to her, Grandpa? Please?"

Grandpa sighed and shook his head, but he finally took the phone. "Liz? Maybe St. Louis isn't such a good idea today. Yes. That sounds better. I'll put Luke to work around here. I have a little painting to do. Good, then we'll see you shortly."

Grandpa put the phone back in its cradle and smiled at Molly. "Lizzie's lonesome, Molly — she's got nothing but men in her family, too. And Ned's on the road so much as it is."

Molly put their dishes in the sink. Grandpa pushed himself away from the table and put on his favorite snapbill cap to cover his bald spot. He hugged Molly on his way outside to wait for Lizzie and Luke.

Molly popped another sweet pickle into her mouth and sat down, wondering. Dresses, phooey. Why did Lizzie want to take Molly shopping for clothes that she didn't need? Didn't she have more serious things to do, right here? And what good would the most beautiful dress in the world be, if Molly lost the Mare?

3

According to Grandpa, Lizzie's new Studebaker Land Cruiser was robin's-egg blue. Lizzie had told Grandpa several times it was officially Capri blue, but Grandpa's mind was made up. The Land Cruiser was a strange-looking car — no other car looked anything like it — and that, Lizzie said, was what she liked about it. The car was pointed at both ends, as if it had two fronts, which made Molly think of deep-sea fish that seemed to have eyes at both ends of their bodies. The robin's-egg Capri blue Studebaker Land Cruiser hummed up the brick driveway. "Hi, Liz; hi, Luke," Grandpa called.

The car stopped under the biggest elm of all, by the back porch. "Hi, Pa," Lizzie said, getting out. She called Grandpa "Pa" and Luke called him "Grandpa," even though he wasn't theirs. Grandpa was Molly's *daddy's* pa; Lizzie was *Mama's* sister. Everybody, even the boys on Grandpa's American

Legion Junior baseball team, called him "Pa" without being related at all.

"Right pretty day, Lizzie. Bet we can talk Molly into a shopping trip." Grandpa whittled on an elm stick and chewed away at his pitcher's cud. When he talked he parked his wad of "t'baccy" in his cheek, like a chipmunk.

Grandpa smiled and gave Lizzie a big wink. "Look here, Molly, all we're going to do here is spatter around some Sherwin-Williams Aluminum. I'm glad you've got old duds on, Luke. This job's going to be messy."

Luke was practicing his move to first, out of the stretch, like some big baseball pitcher, but when he heard that, he stopped midpitch, his eyes huge.

"Wouldn't you sooner keep me company downtown, Molly?" Lizzie said. "We just might find something pretty to wear."

"You're not *just* going to paint. You'll play baseball, too," Molly said. "You'll give him a lesson."

"And what's so terrible about that?" Grandpa said. "Old-timers like me like to feel useful now and then."

Grandpa smiled and shifted a bit on his canvas camp stool. He took off his cap and smoothed the three hairs on top of his damp pink scalp. The elms played shadow tattoos on his bare head, and his round features and kind blue eyes made Molly feel very selfish all of a sudden. This was *her* grandpa, not Luke's.

"Nobody else *I* know gets pitching lessons from

your grandpa," Luke said. Luke's only grandpa lived in Kansas, in a hospital.

"Oh? What do you know about it, Mr. Smarty? What about his team? Maybe he gives *me* secret lessons."

"Girls don't play hardball, Molly." Luke arranged a smug smile on his face.

"Is that right? Well, Luke, Grandpa says there's a first time for everything. How would you like it if I were the first woman pitcher in the big leagues?" Molly had no such intention, but she had to say so just to see what Luke would do.

Luke stuck out his tongue. He looked silly.

"That's enough, you two," Lizzie said. "Look, I'm going over to the grocer's. I'll be back in a jiffy, but you think it over, Molly." Lizzie looked back at Molly. "We could just peek in at Gold's to see what they have," she added.

Lizzie meant to be kind. Sometimes Luke didn't deserve such a nice mother. He could be such a baby, like now. As Lizzie's car hummed back down the driveway bricks, Luke smirked some more and threw his silly little baseball up into the trees. The ball tore off leaves, and they floated down as though it were autumn already.

"Look what you're doing, Luke," Molly said.

"They'll grow more leaves," Luke replied. He kept throwing the ball up in the air.

"Grandpa, please make him stop. They're *our* trees, Luke, not yours."

Luke threw her an angry look.

"Son," Grandpa said, "let's see what you've been doing with your fastball. Got any action on it yet?"

"Sure!" Luke said.

Sure, Molly thought.

"Now take it easy, Luke — you'll knock an old geezer like me right off his pins." Grandpa would handle Luke. Grandpa knew how to get along with people.

Everybody in Comfort knew Robby McAfee because he had been a baseball player. Until she started listening to Harry Carray and the Cardinals' games lately, Molly never realized just how many people knew who Grandpa was. Now, whenever a pitcher got close to a no-hitter, she would hear about Grandpa. Harry Carray and Gabby Street, who had been one of Grandpa's catchers, would talk about the April day in Chicago when Robby McAfee pitched his no-hitter in the second game of a double-header. What seemed really special was that Grandpa had relieved the end of the first game and got credit for winning that one, too. "Two wins in one day," the announcers always said. Hadn't been done before, hadn't been done since. Grandpa? It was hard to believe about this bald, soft-spoken man who chewed his tobacco and whittled out under the elms.

Now Grandpa was trying to make Luke a pitcher, just as he had Daddy, and Luke wanted to be a pitcher in the worst way. Sometimes it bothered Molly — Luke taking over her grandfather like that. Molly couldn't help it that Uncle Ned was always on the road and that Luke needed a man to look up to. Why did they have to shuffle people around so much in this family? Lizzie wanting a little girl. Luke wanting a grandpa or a daddy. Grandpa maybe, wanting another boy to teach to pitch. Well, maybe sharing was all right, but just so everybody understood who was finally whose. Luke might pretend that Grandpa was his, but he knew whose pony the Mare was.

And Molly was worried about the Mare. Not that Daddy would punish the Mare for the Melissa Tyde Show — which was really Molly's fault — but that the Mare might remember the disaster with Luke. Horses had very strange, selective memories. Molly leaned her head next to Grandpa's and whispered in his ear. "Promise me something?" she whispered.

"I can promise you're going to get yourself beaned, Molly. Luke's got no control."

"Grandpa, I'm serious. If Luke wants a ride, he has to wait till I get back. Remember what happened last time."

"Molly, I remember, all right. And you'll be taking first base in a minute. Go on, now. Riding is the last thing on Luke's mind — unless your fussing gives him the idea."

At that moment Luke's idea of a fastball whizzed past Molly's head. She took a quick step back.

"You girls go find a pretty dress, Molly," Grandpa said. "Lizzie knows what's nice, better than your daddy and I do. And you'll have a good time together." Another ball zoomed past Molly.

"You see what I mean?" Grandpa muttered.

29

"High and outside, young fellow," he called to Luke. "Got to get that fastball to break low and stop that sailing." Grandpa chuckled. Luke was having a conniption on his imaginary mound, kicking the grass.

"Run indoors and give that mane a lick and a promise," Grandpa said.

"I didn't say I'd go, yet," Molly pointed out.

"I know," Grandpa said, smiling. "Just in case."

"Let me brush your hair, Molly-o," Mama says.

Her eyes closed, Molly leans back against Mama's legs. She sits on the floor in front of Mama, who is in her favorite chair, the little sewing rocker. Molly loves Mama to brush her hair. Molly's long black curls are difficult for her to brush herself, and Mama's brush strokes pull Molly's head back, gently.

"You have such pretty hair," Mama says. Mama makes Molly feel so special. Pretty, even if she isn't.

Molly smells Mama's grown-up-lady perfume, which comes in fancy crystal bottles from Paris, France. Mama sometimes dabs a cool spot of toilet water on Molly's wrists and behind her ears, and then Molly is grown up, too, and beautiful, like a lady. Like Mama.

Molly opened her eyes.

Grandpa had said the haircut would be a good idea, that the curls were always tangling. They tried braids for a while, but the braids were too much of a problem in the morning, when everybody had to leave the house at once. Nobody ever had time to help Molly with her hair. Daddy tried, but the braids always got soft and fell apart. Molly told him "tighter," but Daddy was afraid he'd hurt her.

Daddy hadn't said anything when he saw the new haircut, but he didn't have to. His eyes said everything. It was a different Molly. It was a Molly who could take care of her own hair. Daddy looked sad, but he looked sad about many things, sad in ways he wouldn't talk about to anyone.

"Your daddy's got a lot on his mind," Graham would say.

But what? Why *couldn't* they talk about things? Molly knew about the problems at the mines — unions and a new law about smoke that meant the mines had to have new equipment to wash the coal, and then there was oil heat, the biggest problem of all. Grandpa was still the president of McAfee Coal Company; Daddy was chief engineer and vice president. Grandpa had those problems on his mind too. Maybe having two jobs was too hard for Daddy.

Molly brushed angrily at her short black curls and wiped a tear off her cheek. Her hair did what it wanted anyway. This awful, ugly short haircut. She should never have agreed to it. Molly thought of brushing the Mare's tail, which she needed to fan flies. It was better for horses when they had a friend around to stand nose-to-tail, nose-to-tail with, fanning each other's faces. Maybe people were the same.

Crying wouldn't change things, or that's what people said.

The Studebaker's horn broke into Molly's thoughts. How easy it would be to stay here, to be a little girl forever, not to have to deal with problems. Dresses. Melissas. Lukes. Haircuts. Phooey.

Out under the elms, Grandpa called, "Molly! Molly-o!"

"Coming," Molly said softly. Grandpa couldn't hear her.

"Lizzie's here, sweetheart," Grandpa called again.

Molly pulled a tissue out of the silver box on Mama's dressing table and blew her nose.

All right, then.

Just this once, Molly would try to be grown up.

4

Lizzie's car smelled so new.

Molly leaned back. She wouldn't get sick, not just going downtown. It was going to St. Louis that always did it — fourteen miles through the hills and down the bluffs. On clear days, the city glistened in the morning sunlight like a toy village for Luke's American Flyer train. That is, if Molly stopped reading long enough to notice. She wasn't much for scenery, especially the Mississippi River.

Lizzie's car's smooth seats were cool against Molly's legs. Molly wished all cars whole, and beautiful — intact and shiny and perfect.

"You're mighty quiet today, Molly. Did I drag you away from something you *really* wanted to do?" Lizzie reached over, giving Molly's arm a little pat.

"No, I decided I needed to shop with you," Molly said. "We'll keep each other company."

"Absolutely!" Lizzie said. "Curious about this

dress-hunting expedition?" Lizzie's smile made Molly think of flowers.

"Well . . . yes," Molly admitted. "I actually don't need a new dress."

"No, you *do* need a dress. Your daddy's going to tell you about a wonderful surprise at dinner tonight." She smiled, driving down Central toward town. "Now don't look at me like that. I gave my word not to tell you. But it is something *very* nice."

"But a dress?" Molly said.

"A dress." Lizzie smiled and shifted gears. "I'm sorry to be the one to tell you, Molly, but life has a few occasions when jeans and a shirt just won't do."

"Oh, I can't wait till suppertime, Lizzie! Just a tiny clue?"

"No, I promised to help you find a dress, and promised not to tell the secret. You'll understand why when Jack tells you. Now, our mission is to find you the prettiest summer dress in Comfort and a pair of white patent leather shoes to go with it. OK?"

"I got new black patents for Easter that I've only worn on Sundays. I really need some new sneakers. I'm not so sure I need this new dress."

"Take my word for it, Molly. You need the dress." Lizzie stretched and leaned behind the Land Cruiser's wheel, looking up and down the block for a parking place. "This will be one very special occasion," she said.

"Oh Lizzie, please — just a little hint?"

"If I did, your daddy would know in a minute.

Ah, look at that! What wonderful luck! A place right across the street from Gold's." Lizzie put the car in reverse and leaned around to survey the parking place. "I hope I can do this — it looks pretty tight."

Molly peered out the window. "OK over here," she said. And then she looked across the street.

No, it wasn't OK at all.

It wasn't the parking spot. It was Melissa Tyde and her mother, just coming out of Gold's front door. Molly scrunched down in the seat. Maybe Melissa wouldn't see her. Maybe they would walk away quickly as Lizzie finished parking. But no. Lizzie was out the door. "Come on, Molly," she said impatiently.

It was too late. "Elizabeth! How are you, darling!" Amanda Tyde waved at Lizzie and Molly. Melissa's mother grabbed her by the hand and came across to the shady side of Central Avenue.

"We're just fine, Amanda, and you? Hello, Melissa. How nice you look in pink."

"We couldn't be better, darling. Of course we haven't been wildly successful here with our shopping, but you know how it is — small-town stores and all."

At first Molly tried to avoid looking at Melissa, but then she thought, What did I do wrong? It was Melissa who had something to be ashamed of, behaving so badly, beating on *her* pony with a crop. Melissa should be the sheepish one. But when Molly raised her eyes she found the other girl glaring at her with her mouth pulled into a tight little smirk, with the corners down. She looked as though she were bored and smelling something very unpleasant at the same time. Melissa carried three parcels: a very large box from Gold's and two other bags. Molly wondered how many packages it took before Melissa's mother would call shopping "wildly successful."

"But don't you find Gold's very accommodating?" Lizzie said to Mrs. Tyde. "They're happy to get whatever you want if they don't have it."

"If you can wait forever!" Mrs. Tyde answered. "Melissa and I are getting ready for our annual two weeks in Charlottesville — Roscoe's family is there, you know — and then Roscoe and I go to Portugal for three weeks, and of course I've got to get this young lady outfitted for camp."

"You're going to camp?" Molly said.

"Sure, aren't you?" Melissa said. "Camp Weehasket. You must have heard of it."

"No," Molly had to say.

"It's near Charlevoix. You know, in Michigan? Really, you haven't heard of it?"

Molly shook her head.

"I'm going for the *whole* month of August. Actually I leave on July twenty-eighth."

Molly took a deep breath. "Well, what about your riding?"

"Oh, they have plenty of horses at camp. *Big* horses."

Dumb ones, too, Molly guessed. Melissa did look

fine, none the worse for this morning's ride. She was fidgeting again, pulling on her mother the way she had been pulling on Dr. Tyde this morning. "Can't we *go* now?" she asked.

"In a minute, dear," her mother said, turning back to Lizzie. "And how is your bridge foursome these days, Elizabeth, dear?" Beautiful Mrs. Tyde smiled a perfect smile, and Molly saw lipstick smeared on her perfect front teeth.

Melissa stuck out her lip. "Don't look at me like that!" she hissed. Molly didn't know she was looking at Melissa any particular way at all, so she turned her head and looked across the street at the front of Heilemann's Hardware. Two bright blue push mowers flanked the front entrance, a stalk of rakes by one and a stalk of brooms by the other.

"You think you're really something," Melissa whispered, "and you think your pony is pretty hot stuff. Well, Molly McAfee, just because I'm going to camp, don't think you've heard the last of Melissa Tyde. When we Tydes make up our minds about something, Molly, that is *it*. Your little tricks won't stop me. You can just go whisper *that* in your dumb horse's ear."

Molly could feel her face growing hot with anger. Melissa was such a brat. Molly wanted nothing more to do with her, or her beautiful mother.

"Look, I'm sorry about what happened," Molly said.

"Who cares? My daddy will do anything I tell

37

him. Including buying that dumb little pony, *if* I feel like it. It might not be worth the trouble, though it would serve you right, Molly."

How could she deal with a person like Melissa? It wouldn't work to beg Melissa not to buy the Mare. Melissa would just be all the more determined. Oh, why hadn't Melissa gone to Camp Sillybasket for the months of June and July as well if it was such a terrific place? Then this would never have happened.

Lizzie, why are you talking forever and forever to awful Mrs. Tyde?

Why had they run into them like this?

Why don't you get lost, Melissa? Any desert island will do.

Why did Molly need this new dress? Why was she here?

There were a million whys.

"Come along, Melissa, dear," Mrs. Tyde said at last. What people said about Amanda Tyde was true — she *was* the most beautiful woman in Comfort, even with lipstick on her teeth. Her way of talking mesmerized people, no matter what she was saying. She was tall and blond and tan, with bangle bracelets that clinked together as she finally shifted her packages to her other arm and said, "So wonderful to see you, Elizabeth. Do have a marvelous, exciting summer, darling." Melissa's mother checked her beautiful reflection in the store window and walked off.

Molly wondered about that. How could Lizzie's plain old summer begin to compare with the

Tydes'? That hadn't been a nice thing to say, no matter how good it sounded on the surface.

The Tydes walked away, and Melissa looked back over her shoulder at Molly and stuck out her tongue.

They had a motto at Gold's: "If we don't have it, we'll get it." And they did. They got Molly her black velvet helmet for jumping the Mare, and on special order from New York City, her canary riding breeches, like Melissa's, and the hacking jacket made of Scottish tweed.

Gold's was like several stores. First you come to ladies' handbags, gloves, and hankies. Straight ahead were linens and household goods; on the left all down one wall were fabrics of every kind imaginable: silks and satins and laces, cotton and gingham and swiss and piqué, and velveteen and corduroy and wool and tweed, and huge tubes of upholstery. On the right was the men's department, where Molly and Mama used to shop for Daddy and Grandpa, for shirts and ties, handkerchiefs and socks. Farther back the dark red carpet started, where men in vests with pins in their mouths put cuffs on pants. There was a spittoon for people like Grandpa.

Today Lizzie led the way to Ladies' and Children's Ready-to-Wear, which was a separate part, up three steps and off beyond the yard goods. And here everything — whether on shelves or hangers or in boxes — was behind glass. All the dresses were in magical glass closets. You needed a saleslady to release secret catches, and then doors came open and whole racks of clothes would roll out, rustling.

Mama's wedding dress rises in a misty cloud.

Today the dress hangs in Gold's Bridal Salon, which is really only a special glass cabinet at the back with all the fanciest formals and best afternoon dresses.

An Oriental carpet covers the floor. Here is a sofa, and here a chair and a lamp and a coffee table with issues of Vogue *and* Harper's Bazaar *on it. This is where Mama comes to the spring and fall fashion shows.*

But today Mama has come to buy her wedding gown. She is very sorry to say that nothing she sees is exactly right. Everything is just too fancy, too fussy. Mama wants something simple. Something classic, Mama says — something that will look good forever. A dress her daughter — if she has a daughter someday — might want to get married in, too. No, this one has entirely too much lace for me, Mama says. Sorry, too busy.

One day, Mama says to Molly, you may want to wear it. If you like — if you feel *like getting married.*

That is the way Mama talks. With Mama you never *have to do anything; you do things because you want to, because you have a good reason to or because you really feel like it.*

Molly supposes she will one day get married, though she doesn't have anyone in mind yet.

The dress department smells wonderful.

Mama's wedding dress's compartment in her closet always smells beautiful, like a room full of flowers.

Molly floats, closes her eyes, drifts on a perfume that wafts in from another time, one that is, like the dress, much simpler. Safer.

Perhaps too simple, too perfect, too safe.

"Molly!" Mama is furious! Molly has never seen her like this, never.

Lightning snaps from her eyes, and Molly wants to run and hide, like a baby afraid of a storm.

"Mama, Mama," Molly says. "I didn't mean it, Mama. Please don't be angry. It was an accident, the girl falling, cutting her knee."

"How could you?" Mama says. "You hurt her. What in the world made you push that girl back like that?"

"But Mama," Molly says, "I didn't mean for her to fall. I didn't mean for her to get hurt. *She pushed me first." Molly doesn't know how to make Mama understand. If only there were some way, but Mama seems not to want to listen.*

"Two wrongs don't make a right, Molly," Mama says, "and you didn't fix things by pushing her too. You only made things much, much worse."

"No, you don't understand," Molly says, again and again. But no matter how many times she says it, it doesn't help.

"Molly, I'm ashamed of you. You have to think before you act," Mama says.

If only Mama hadn't said — that is the worst of all. Mama ashamed of her.

Molly is glad no one else hears Mama say that awful thing.

It is time for Mama to go. There is no more time to talk.

Mama gets her purse from the hall table, gives Molly a quick, disappointed look. "Now we're late," Mama says. "You have to go back to school and I'm late now for my appointment, Molly. I have to go to St. Louis.

"I'll be back by five," Mama says.

"We'll talk when I get back," Mama says.

Mrs. Simmons beamed at Molly and held up a white dress — all eyelet, with pale pink organdy underneath. The holey flowers crawling all over the dress trailed from one side to the other, from shoulder to hem. Around the waist a wide white sash was trimmed with two tiny pink ribbons and a nosegay of pink fake flowers pinned on a bow. Ruffled sleeves jutted from each shoulder. Molly thought it was a terrible dress, and she bet it itched, too.

"What do you think, dear?" Mrs. Simmons asked her.

"I suppose it's a pretty dress," Molly said, "but it's a little complicated. For me, I mean."

Mrs. Simmons looked at her thoughtfully, then her smile returned. "Yes, something a bit simpler." She turned to Lizzie and sighed, "Poor sweet darling, she's the picture of her mother."

Why did people always have to say things like that? Molly *wasn't* the picture of her mother. She was nowhere near the picture of her mother! Mama was beautiful and grown up; Molly was a gawky little girl, and not at all pretty, besides. And as for dresses, well, Molly would rather wear jeans and talk to her too-little, too-fat pony. If only she could tell Mrs. Simmons that.

"Do you really think so?" Lizzie was saying. "We always thought she favored Jack." Lizzie smiled, but she looked as if getting Molly this dress was serious business.

"Oh, Mr. McAfee's coloring to a T, but her mother's ways, absolutely," Mrs. Simmons said. "And now that I know what you want, Molly, I have just the thing for you."

Daddy would tell her tonight. That's what Lizzie said. She would just have to wait. But so long? What was this dress for?

Mrs. Simmons took the awful eyelet back through a door next to the bridal department.

Can it be? It isn't impossible. Five years is long enough. Molly is afraid. Afraid she knows, afraid she can see everything.

A wedding.

In the case by the door a wedding dress comes to life. It is a long white dress with lace ruffles and beads sparkling all over it, complicated by pearls and streamers and a preposterous, wide train and a headdress that balloons out a yard all around.

Somehow Molly knows it is night. The store is closed; the only customers are Molly and her daddy.

Molly thinks, What if the surprise is a wedding,

one in which her daddy is the groom? Not the wedding with Mama. Another one. Everything in this dream is becoming clear, like crystal, though a mist swirls around Molly's head like the veil around the bride's. So that is why Lizzie is getting Molly a special dress — so she can be part of the wedding.

A voice from somewhere says: Yes, your mother is really and truly dead. Time to go on with another mother. Forget about the real one, once and for all.

How could Daddy? How could he forget? Molly is furious.

It can't be so. Don't people go on dates first? Does Daddy go on secret dates when he says he is going hunting or fishing?

The figure in the wedding dress case stirs.

Its arm moves. It is coming to life!

The bride-figure moves again; this time the whole body turns.

It raises a white kid glove and taps on the glass, as if it wants to get out of the cabinet.

Mama? Is that you?

No.

Mama would open the door and just walk out, and that would be that, no foolishness.

Who, then? The face is shrouded by layers and layers of netting wound around, like an old-fashioned beekeeper.

Who is it? An ugly witch? A wicked stepmother?

Daddy might not mean to do such a thing. It

*might be an accident, a trick. Daddy is blinded,
fooled by his sadness.*

*The door of the cabinet swings open. The
woman in white steps out.*

*For a moment, Molly stands frozen. Then she
knows what she must do; she has to know who this
woman is. She will unmask this spy, this traitor,
this impostor. Daddy will see his mistake.*

*Daddy dozes in his chair. He works too hard.
Molly rushes at the figure in white.*

"Molly, you can't be in the market for one of
those yet." Lizzie laughed. Molly was holding the
veil of the bride's headdress. The lace edging was
scratchy in her fingers.

Her face burned.

"Molly, dear, I'm so sorry—we got to talking,"
Mrs. Simmons said. "Now tell me, what do you
think of *this* dress?"

Mrs. Simmons held up another white dress, an
entirely different white dress. This one was made of
ribbed piqué, with a big square sailor collar both in
front and in back. It had no sleeves at all and its
gathered skirt was not too full, but full enough. Best
of all, there were no ribbons or flowers or ruffles or
embroidered holes anywhere.

It was just right.

"Yes," Molly said. "This is my dress." For whatever the occasion was.

5

Directly across the street from Gold's was Kammerer's Candy Shop, and Lizzie's robin's-egg blue car had the parking place right in front of Kammerer's door. On a slate in the window was printed FRESH PEACH. How Molly would love an ice cream cone. Maybe, she thought, after Susskind's. Lizzie was going to insist on going to Susskind's for shoes.

Lizzie slid the dress box through the car's open window. "Can you believe there are places in St. Louis where you have to lock your car?" she said. "A day like this, you close up a car and it would be an oven!"

It *was* hot. Molly saw the heat rising in wavy lines from the concrete. Tonight's *Comfort Evening Star* might have the picture of somebody frying an egg on one of these downtown sidewalks. The paper did that at least once every summer.

"We'll only be a minute at Susskind's," Lizzie promised.

But just then a little bell tinkled, the door to Kammerer's opened, and an icy blast of air-conditioning blew out.

"Well, what a small world!" a familiar voice said. Without turning around Molly knew. It was Amanda Tyde.

When she turned, there they were, and Melissa might as well have been sticking out her tongue again. They looked cool and refreshed. Molly was hot and tired and ready to go home and stand under the sprinkler with the Mare. "Hi, Molly," Melissa said, with a strange emphasis on the *hi*.

"Darlings, you've simply got to have some of Kammerer's fresh peach. Elizabeth, dear, it's simply out of this world!"

"*I* had the Fresh Peach Shortcake Supreme," Melissa said.

Oh, you would, Molly thought.

"It was absolutely scrummmmptious!!" Melissa said. "If you want any of that peach, you'd better *hurry* before they run *out*, Molly."

"Melissa sweet, some people have better things to do than sit in ice cream parlors. It looks as though you found something at Gold's, Elizabeth."

"Yes, Molly found a lovely dress."

"At *Gold's?*" Melissa said, incredulous.

Yes, at *Gold's.* "Mrs. Simmons knows what I like," Molly said, not knowing where that came from.

"Well, I guess. I never can find anything there I'd care to drag home, but next time I'll ask for Mrs. Simmons."

Lizzie managed a smile, finally, and turned to Mrs. Tyde. "Amanda, we must run. We have one more stop before we treat ourselves to Kammerer's. Take care, now, and have a good trip to Virginia."

Melissa and her mother, chattering and whispering, walked off toward the square, where Mrs. Tyde said their driver was waiting. A driver. Really, Molly thought. Lizzie waited till she was sure the Tydes were out of earshot. "What a snotty little girl!" she said. "Is she always like that?"

"As far as I know," Molly answered.

"But Pa said the Tydes had asked about the Mare for Melissa. What happened? No one said anything."

"Melissa and her father came to see the Mare this morning. Dr. Tyde is an expert rider himself. I hope they forget about it, but you never can tell about Melissa. She seems determined."

"And?"

"And I don't know." Lizzie linked arms with Molly as they started for Susskind's.

"Maybe it's just a passing whim, Molly," Lizzie suggested. "Maybe you shouldn't worry about her."

"Oh, I have to worry. There's a part I didn't tell you — Melissa rode the Mare this morning."

"Well naturally, Molly. If she's serious about buying her, that makes perfect sense."

"Yes, but Melissa had a crop."

"Oh?"

"And she used it, and the Mare didn't take too kindly to it."

"And the Mare . . ."

"Yes."

"Well, then, that's the end of it for Melissa."

"I thought so too, but you don't know Melissa. She's furious."

"Oh, she'll lose interest, Molly. She has plenty to keep her busy this summer."

"Melissa says she can make her daddy buy the Mare, just to show me. And then what? The Mare will die, either of boredom or abuse. I just know it."

"I see the problem, Molly." Lizzie stopped and gave Molly's shoulders a squeeze. "Look, Molly, you just have to figure out some way to stop Melissa from wanting the Mare. Or else think of a sure way to convince your daddy you have to keep her."

"Oh, Lizzie, I've begged Daddy. All he'll say is it's wrong to keep a pony just to get fat. Even Grandpa says the Mare should go to somebody who'll ride her."

"Let's give it some thought, Molly," Lizzie said. They had reached the shady tile entryway to Susskind's, where, in the horseshoe-shaped window, stiff still plaster ladies wore the latest. "Maybe if you can think of a way that you can put the Mare to work . . . something's sure to come to you."

"But what?"

The next thing she knew, Molly had on a pair of white patent Mary Janes. "You can't wear black shoes with a white piqué dress in the middle of summer," Lizzie assured her as Mr. Susskind wrapped their purchase.

The shoes were just a minor problem. Perhaps she could think up some reason to return them since they seemed so unnecessary. She could claim that they pinched, but she had stepped upon the big machine at Susskind's that saw through your shoes and showed your bones green and could tell definitely whether you were fibbing about how the shoes fit. "My Truth Machine," Mr. Susskind called it. He flashed a gold-rimmed smile that seemed to Molly slightly wicked. Mr. Susskind always made you feel he knew much more than you did or ever could. Him and his Truth Machine!

Driving home, after the fresh peach, Lizzie started singing her favorite song, "Bye, Bye, Blackbird."

"Pack up all your care and woe, here I go, winging low . . ."

"Make my bed, light the light." Molly joined in. Lizzie's smile made the world seem right, and she started singing harmony. Molly sang on, wondering how you packed up woes. Wondering about Melissa. And whether there would be a wedding.

When they turned in at Molly's drive, Grandpa and Luke were still painting the pump. It was almost all new-silver color. Grandpa looked up and saw their bundles. "Looks like you two had a successful hunt," he said. "How about a glass of iced tea, Liz?"

Molly knew Lizzie would say yes, and then Grandpa and Lizzie would visit, talking about things that Molly often didn't completely understand.

Molly raced up the stairs to her room and put the box from Gold's on her bed.

Was her heart pounding from racing upstairs like that? Or was she actually excited about a *dress?*

Gold's dark blue box had a white ribbon printed on it, the way you tie birthday presents, around the corners. In the upper left, next to a forever-tied white printed bow, a tag in flowing writing said "Gold's" and then "Fine Ladies' Ready-to-Wear." Molly and Mama had laughed about the Gold's boxes — Molly said they needed a gold-colored box, and Mama said, "Aren't we 'fine ladies,' Molly?" Mama could always find jokes in words. Molly had loved her games and riddles and puzzles.

Now Molly lifted the lid carefully. A sticker that looked just like Gold's outside tag fastened the puffy white tissue paper. As Molly broke the seal, the tissue rustled like an unfolding secret. There was the dress. Molly took it out carefully and laid it across her bed: white on white, the dress on the chenille spread with its loops of flowers garlanding the edges of the bed. Molly unwrapped Mr. Susskind's Truth Machine white patentleather Mary Janes and took the wads of white tissue out of the toes. Side by side she set the shoes below the dress, in the place where her feet might be if she were lying there like an Egyptian princess. Molly, the mummy-girl. Molly-to-be.

The sun went in. The afternoon turned suddenly cool. Outside Molly's window, the pear tree's leaves moved not at all. It was going to rain, she knew.

Grandpa would say something positive, like they could use this break in the weather.

The Mare, at least, would be glad. She loved nothing better than to stand in a summer rain, letting large drops pelt her dusty back. Rain was the only kind of bath acceptable to the Mare. After Molly would wash the Mare down with a hose, she'd always go find a dusthole to roll in. "Don't let it bother you, Molly," Daddy told her. "That's just how horses are."

And, Molly wondered, how are daddies? What should we expect from them?

"Wait for me," Mollie cries, "please!"

The Mare trots faster and ever faster. Molly is frightened. If only Mama and Daddy didn't have such big horses, they wouldn't go so fast and the Mare wouldn't have to trot like a fool to catch up with them. Faster and faster the Mare trots.

"Kick her," Daddy shouts, "give that little devil a kick. She'll trot like that all day if you let her, Molly."

But how can she? Molly can't. No matter how much she wants to, she simply can't. It will hurt the Mare. Daddy says it won't if she does it gently, the way he's showed her.

Mama nudges her big horse, Ducat, just enough to send him into a rack. It was better, Molly thinks, when she could just ride up behind Mama on Ducat. She didn't have to steer, she didn't have to watch for cars, and she had Mama to hold on to.

The big bay racks on, side to side. Ducat's favorite gait is one of his extra ones — he has five instead of three. The Mare, Daddy says, only has one: trot. Trot, fast trot, faster trot.

Clip-clip-clip-clip. The Mare's tiny feet sound on the hard-packed dirt of the road.

"Molly, make her canter," Mama calls to her. "Pull her head one way and kick with the other heel."

Molly pulls, but she doesn't think she should kick the Mare. She doesn't want to hurt her. The Mare turns and winds around in a circle, confused, making Molly dizzy and frightened.

"I swear to heaven," Daddy says, "what a pair! They take the cake."

"Patience, Jack," Mama says. "Try it again, Molly. Maybe from a walk. She might like that better."

"What if she rears?" Molly asks. "Or bucks?"

"She won't."

Mama is right; the pony doesn't. How does she know these things?

"Be careful, Molly!" Luke calls. "Remember what happened to me." What does Luke know? He sees too many cowboy movies in which many a horse turns maverick. Luke doesn't know about horses; he knows about baseball. No one can know everything, except Mama.

Molly turns the Mare's head a little to the right and nudges her a little with her left heel and squeezes with her legs.

Molly and the Mare go flying down the dirt

road, three beats instead of four. One-two-three,
one-two-three, cantering!

Mama didn't see that. No, Mama never saw the
Mare. Mama and Daddy and Molly, riding together
on a summer evening — that was only one of
Molly's dreams. If only Mama could see Molly can-
tering the Mare out in the open on a road like that.
If only Mama had seen Molly take the Mare over
coops and oxers. If only Molly could have talked to
Mama some more. So many "if onlys." If only
Molly could make Mama proud of her.

The dress was there on the bed. Molly wondered
what time it was. The Baby Ben wasn't ticking. It
said 9:45, but it hadn't been wound since the second
to last day of school. Molly turned away from the
window and the pear tree and started downstairs.

Daddy and Grandpa were talking in the study.
They'd left the door slightly ajar.

Where had Lizzie gone, Molly wondered, and
Luke? Molly had rushed upstairs and hadn't even
thanked Lizzie for taking her shopping, and for the
fresh peach ice cream cone. Disappearing, though,
wasn't like Lizzie. Something was going on around
here — lots of things, it seemed.

Molly stood silently against the wall outside the
study door. No matter how hard she tried, she
couldn't exactly make out what Daddy was telling
Grandpa. Something about the mines. She didn't
need to listen to know that. Whenever they talked in
the study, it was something about the mines: unions
or railroads or the price of coal.

Every day Daddy went from one mine to the next making sure everything was all right, that everyone did his job properly, that nothing had gone wrong. Molly wanted to go down into the mines, but Daddy said no, "Mines are dangerous places." Sometimes Molly thought Daddy didn't like the mines much at all but that he didn't have a choice. The mines had been his grandpa's and now they were his daddy's and one day they would be his. And then, Molly guessed, one day hers. Not like the wedding dress, *if* she wanted. Whether she wanted or not.

But the talk Molly heard was different from usual. Daddy's voice had a different edge. He was upset, and his talking was growing louder. "I don't know how it could have happened," Daddy said. "I swear to God I don't."

Molly edged closer to the door, wanting to peek into the slice of lamplight that cut into the hall.

"He got prompt medical attention," Grandpa said. "That's the important thing." But Grandpa sounded as though he were trying to convince himself, too.

"You're positive he hasn't regained consciousness?" Grandpa asked.

"Not yet."

"That's not good, you know." Grandpa did know about things like that. Grandpa was going to be a doctor — he had finished with medical school and had begun his internship when the big leagues swept him away. Then the family wanted him back home in Comfort, to run the coal business. When

Grandpa talked to Molly about medical school he would shake his head. She could tell he always wished he'd been a doctor, anyway.

Daddy said, "Doc Beckman says all we can do is wait. There's nothing else to do in these cases, he says."

"Henry's right. I know he's doing everything he can for Haller. Oh, I feel *terrible* about this."

"I think I should go see Haller's wife," Daddy said. "His kids will probably be at the hospital too." He paused, then said, "This isn't going to be easy."

"Shall I come with you, son?"

There was a silence. Daddy must have shook his head no. "I'll be back late," he said. "Don't wait supper for me."

"Where's Molly?" Grandpa asked.

As quietly as she could, Molly retraced her steps back down the hall. She got halfway up the stairs before Daddy called "Molly!" from the study door.

"Here I am."

"I have to go, Molly," he said. "We had an accident at the mine on Cornwallis Road — one of the men is hurt. Apparently Horace, that mule you like, kicked one of the men. The man's in the hospital, hurt pretty badly."

What? Molly thought. Horace? "I don't believe that, not for one minute," she said, surprising herself.

"Molly, what's got into you?" Grandpa said, coming to the door behind Daddy.

"I just don't believe that. Horace is the gentlest mule there is. Don't you remember last summer?

How could a mule like that hurt anybody? It's a lie!"

"Slow down, firecracker," Daddy said. "To tell you the truth, I find it hard to believe myself. But even a steady animal like Horace — you never can tell what might set them off."

"Maybe I'll just ask Horace what really happened," Molly said. "I bet his side of the story is different."

Grandpa slammed his *Globe-Democrat* down so hard Molly thought the table would collapse. She had never seen him do that. "Enough of that kind of talk, young lady." He stalked out to the kitchen and ran himself a glass of water. Molly shivered. Then Grandpa came to the end of the hall. "You're talking foolishness, Molly, and this is a serious situation," he said. "No one's in the mood for such silly talk."

Grandpa went out onto the back screened porch and sat, looking at nothing. What had happened to Grandpa?

"Pa's worried, honey," Daddy said. He brushed Molly's curls away from her eyes. "The man who is hurt may die. It's a serious injury — his head. He's still unconscious."

"And that's why Lizzie and Luke went home?"

Daddy nodded.

"But Lizzie said you had a secret to tell me. Will you still? Please?"

"Molly, sweetheart, it's too complicated. I have to go to the hospital. I don't have time to explain it now."

"Oh, Daddy," Molly said.

Actually, Daddy's answer wasn't any answer at all, Molly thought. Whatever it was, he could tell her in three minutes if he wanted to. Daddy wasn't keeping his word. Daddy was always taking things back — the pony, and now this secret. Everything was so snarled up — the Mare, Melissa, the dress, the surprise, and now the accident. It was like an old piece of forgotten knitting, with the yarn so tangled it would never be a sweater.

The mules stand in a tight knot at the far end of the pond pasture. There are twenty of them, ten pair, and they are on top for the summer months, when work in the mine slows down and only a few animals are kept underground at any one time. In the summer no one needs much coal, and some of the mines close down altogether.

Mules are ugly. Or so Molly used to think. They may be the same general shape as horses, but mules aren't pretty. Those washed-out-looking undersides and their huge ugly faces and long bony legs and craggy heads. And those ridiculous ears. But even if they aren't pretty, Molly feels sorry for the mules and knows how glad they are when summer comes and they can take a rest from hauling coal, deep down in a hole in the ground where it is always night, always damp, and nothing but work. Molly likes to watch the mules being brought up. They need a few minutes to get used to the light, but they are frisky and know now is the time for some fun.

On evenings when Daddy does the evening feeding, when the night man is off or not there for some reason, Daddy takes her with him. Molly takes the mules carrots, secretly, under her shirt.

Horace, the biggest and boniest mule of all, is the friendliest. The mules in the McAfee mines have funny names because Mr. Slade, their breeder, likes Greek and Latin. He named them Ulysses and Plato, Aristotle and Sappho, Hero and Orpheus, Juno and Euripides. And Horace.

Horace trots out from the group of mules and snuffles Molly's hand with his wet face.

A carrot?

A sugar cube?

The other mules make their half-squeak, half-honk noises like a gang of bad boys laughing at him. But Horace pays no mind. He comes to stand by the gate and say hello, and Molly climbs up the planks to his back, and Horace walks slowly around and around the pasture.

Daddy comes out of the stable. "Molly! Get down from there!" he says. "Are you crazy, riding that mule like that? Come here, Horace."

"Daddy, it's all right. Horace likes me. See how gentle he is? I don't even need a bridle."

"I see. I see, all right. Hold still, Horace. Now you get off, Molly."

Horace looks around and sniffs Molly's sneaker. Then he edges close to the fence, as if to help Molly find the easiest way down.

"See, Daddy," Molly says, "isn't he a wonderful old mule? He's smart, isn't he?"

"*Some people say mules are smarter than horses,*" Daddy allows, "*and some people think horse sense is better than people sense.*"

"*You see, he's so gentle,*" Molly says, patting Horace's nose softly.

"*He is one of the best, Molly. A real steady, smart mule. More than I can sometimes say for a certain girl I know.*"

"*Oh, Daddy,*" Molly says. She jumps from the fence onto Daddy's neck with a huge hug. At least Daddy isn't angry anymore.

6

Molly lay very still.

Her eyes were closed, but she was wide awake.

She counted the cars passing on Central Avenue and paid close attention to each one's sound. Was this one Daddy's, coming back from the hospital? That one? No. Not yet.

At last a car turned into the brick drive, climbed the driveway hill, and went into the garage.

He was home. Molly heard Daddy slide the garage door shut. She heard the crunch of his feet on the gravel walk as he came up to the house.

Molly kept her eyes closed tight. She counted the five steps to the back porch as Daddy climbed them. She heard the back screen door opening, the spring singing high and tight, and then, far away downstairs, a muffled hello. Grandpa was waiting on the back porch, where he had sat all this while. Molly had told him good-night, and Grandpa's anger had passed, at least. It had only been a few hours earlier. It seemed like a year ago.

Molly peeked over at Baby Ben, which she had set at 9:15. The luminous spots and wands of pale green said 11:10. Molly heard more quiet voices. Then Grandpa said, "Oh no!" He sounded as if someone had hit him in the stomach. Molly knew why Daddy had been so late. The man had died.

It would be Horace's fault.

Molly cried and pulled the sheet over her eyes. Why did it have to happen? Why did any accident have to happen?

After a bit, Molly's door edged open, at first just a crack. Then it opened farther, letting in the faint orange of the light down the hall. The top of Daddy's head appeared, and then his eyes.

"Daddy?" Molly said. "You got home."

"I didn't mean to wake you, Molly."

"You didn't, Daddy. I was waiting for you."

"All alone, in the dark?" Daddy said. He opened the door all the way. "I'll tuck you in."

When Daddy gave Molly her hug and kiss, she felt that his cheeks were hot and damp. Had he been crying, too?

"The man isn't all right," Molly said.

"No, Molly. He died." Even the words sounded heavy, like huge rocks falling.

"I'm sorry," Molly said. She couldn't think of anything else.

"Yes, me too," Daddy said, his face in the dark. Molly reached up and snapped on the reading light over her headboard so she could see his face. "You ought to sleep now, Molly. You can read tomorrow." He didn't understand.

"What happened, Daddy?"

"It was an accident, Molly, just an accident. No one knows why accidents happen."

"But Horace didn't really hurt the man, did he?"

"I don't know," Daddy said.

"You won't believe them if they say that, will you? Daddy, you know that can't be true."

"No."

"So you don't believe it, do you?"

"No, I don't believe it."

"Good," Molly said, "because neither do I. I may not know what happened exactly, but I *know* Horace." She turned off the light.

"Yes you do," Daddy said, folding back the top hem of her sheet. "Time for sleep, Molly," he said. Outside, the crickets sang a frantic song of summer and night. Daddy kissed Molly's cheek, and as he disappeared into the orange that slowly edged out of her room, Molly wondered: Did the man have children? What did he say when he said good-night to them?

When morning did come, it was gray. After the thunder threatening all yesterday afternoon and the heat lightning all last evening, the rain fell while Molly slept, as the radio had predicted. It wasn't the kind of rain that came and went and left you clean and fresh. It was a rain that hung around in the air, like some boring guest you wished would go home. The *Farmer's Almanac* predicted a wet summer, and Grandpa claimed the *Farmer's Almanac* was generally right, at least as long as he'd been consulting it for his garden.

Molly, barely able to walk, wanders among the giant rhubarb plants. Their huge flat leaves spread out on pink stems, like clumps of small, tropical, low-lying trees.

Molly knows that toad is here somewhere.

There *he goes! Into the strawberries! Molly stumbles up and down Grandpa's strawberry hills, scuffling through the straw that covers the ground.*

"Molly!" Mama sings out over the backyard into the field. "Molly-o, where are you?" Mama calls.

Now the toad is gone, lost forever in the strawberries and rhubarb. Molly turns and runs to the house on short, fat legs, fast, to Mama, where it is safe and nothing is lost for good.

Daddy looked up from his coffee cup. His dark tanned forehead, the skin shiny and tight, was piled up in a row of perfectly even furrows that stretched all the way across his face. "Make a frown, Daddy," Molly used to say, because she liked to touch the wrinkles that felt like a doll's washboard. But this wasn't a frown for fun. Daddy's eyes looked bruised and tired and pink-edged, as though he hadn't slept much.

Nobody ever beat Daddy to the breakfast table; at the drop of a hat Daddy would tell you that nobody had for years. Usually Daddy had a smile, a hug, and a "Morning, Molly." But now this terrible look clouded his face and brought that storm of wrinkles to his forehead. His mouth was a perfectly straight line, held tight and thin, and his blue eyes retreated into a squint.

"Daddy?" Molly said.

"Hi, Molly." Daddy forced a smile and shook his head and pursed his lips. He made a sound with his mouth, kind of a kiss, that sounded like disbelief and regret, and shook his head some more. "Did you get right to sleep last night?"

"Yes," Molly lied. "I kept wondering, though, about the man, and Horace."

"You mustn't dwell on it, Molly. However awful it is, it's something that can't be changed. The man didn't know. He didn't regain consciousness. Haller wasn't very old, actually — in fact, one of his children is a girl about your age."

"Haller? Elaine Haller? It was *her* daddy?"

"Yes, Elaine. Do you know her?"

"Sort of. Not well. I know who she is, is all. Is there something I should do, do you think?"

"We'll see. Maybe you can make some special effort for Elaine, even if you aren't best friends. It will help her if you try to be kind right now. Her family's going to have some hard times. There will be a fund for them, and the union benefits, but a widow with those young children — whatever they get won't go far enough." Daddy shook his head. "It's just terrible."

"Do you know anything more about the accident, Daddy? Was it really Horace's fault?"

"That's what they tell me. Horace was the only mule around where Haller was working. They say Horace acted up."

"That doesn't sound like Horace."

"I have to admit, it doesn't. Of all the mules,

Horace is the last I'd expect any trouble from. Always steady as a rock." Daddy blew across the top of his coffee cup. "What I can't get clear is *exactly* what Horace did."

"He wasn't mean, Daddy. He was friendly."

"I know." Daddy stirred a teaspoon and a half of sugar into his cup of coffee. "Have I already put sugar in this?" he asked himself out loud. "My mind's a thousand miles away."

"What will happen, Daddy, to Horace?"

"You mustn't worry yourself about that, Molly. If Horace did something wrong, we have to know so it won't happen again." Daddy reached one of his long arms over toward her, and Molly went into his hug. "How's this: I'll do some fishing around, keep my ears open, see what I can find out." Daddy stopped, listening. "Hush, now — here comes Pa. The accident has him beside himself. Let's be talking about something else."

"Hmmmph," the old man said when he got to the kitchen door. Grandpa seemed weary this morning too, and grumpy. His fringe of hair was mussed, and he said "Hmmmph" again. His step didn't have any spring. He shuffled to the cupboard and got out a cereal bowl, a juice glass, a cup and saucer, and he fished a spoon out of the silverware drawer. He opened another cupboard and got out his bran. "You ought to be eating this stuff, Molly, instead of that puffed wheat you gobble up. Nothing but pure air, that stuff."

"It's good, Grandpa."

"Sure it is, with all that sugar you put on it.

That's going to rot your teeth right out of your head, young lady, and one day you'll wake up and have false teeth like mine. Some things you just never can tell people."

Grandpa raised his eyebrows and gave Daddy an odd look. What was that supposed to mean? Was it about the big secret Daddy should have told her last night? Or was it something Grandpa tried to tell Daddy that *he* hadn't listened to? Molly didn't understand adults and their guessing games, their games of hide-and-seek.

"How many times do I have to tell you, Molly?" Daddy says. "You have to sit very *quiet. A squirrel won't come within a mile if you keep fidgeting like that."*

Molly doesn't want the squirrels to come within a mile. That is *the whole idea.*

If she keeps stirring around, swatting at mosquitoes — real or pretend — scratching at bites, scuffling in the leaves, snapping twigs with her steps, and talking on and on about nothing, then when they go home tonight Daddy's game bag will be empty. Molly knows that will make Daddy glum and sour-faced. He will complain about having a bad day in the woods and tell Grandpa all kinds of stories about how much trouble Molly was.

But she doesn't care.

Molly prefers squirrels alive, not for dinner. Molly hates it when they have squirrel for dinner, no matter how much Daddy and Grandpa may enjoy it. Squirrel tastes different — salty and me-

tallic — no matter how Graham cooks it. Molly can't make the leap, in her mind, from those playful animals in the treetops — chattering, scolding birds — to this. Molly can't watch when Daddy pulls the trigger. Nor will she watch when he cleans squirrels for Graham to cook. "Dressing" is what he calls it, and Molly thinks that the word is all wrong. Backward. She has seen Daddy take the squirrels' fur off like little suits.

"Time to get dressed," Grandpa was saying. "Got to get cracking, make hay while the sun shines." Grandpa always said that, every morning. But this morning he didn't sound at all energetic, just impatient. Annoyed with everything.

"Things will be all right, Grandpa," Molly said. "I'm sorry about the man. Mr. Haller."

"Yes, it's a terrible thing. Younger than your daddy, you know. Haller's father, old Al, used to work in the mines too. A good miner, old Al. Honest as the day is long, and just as hard-working. I was sorry to see him go."

"What happened to him? Did he die?"

"No, he retired, moved away, took the wife and went down somewhere — Arkansas or southern Missouri — to live with a daughter. Someplace off in the Ozarks. I remember old Al telling me what pretty country it was down there." Grandpa shook his head. "The problem is, before he left old Al said to me, 'Now you take good care of my boy.' And I said that I would. Now how am I going to face him?"

"Come on, Pa," Daddy said, "you couldn't have stopped an accident like that from happening. Old Al knows mines. He can't hold you responsible for an accident like this. He knows what kind of life it is — nobody should know better than Al Haller."

"I can't help it, Jack. I feel I let him down."

"That's wrong. He didn't mean you had to look out for his son personally. You're only one man, Pa. People have to look out for themselves, first. There are limits, you know."

Daddy sounded angry. He ran his hand through his thick black curls and drank the rest of his coffee. He didn't eat all of his toast, Molly noticed. "Go get dressed, Molly," he said. "Your pony needs water and hay. Hurry on, now."

Molly had no doubts: Daddy's tone meant she should make herself scarce.

"I guess this changes everything," Daddy said.

Grandpa looked up, his face a question.

"I mean, we can't very well go ahead with the big event, as planned," Daddy said. "It just wouldn't look right."

"I don't see what this has to do with Mary."

"Molly, I told you to get along," Daddy said, sounding very stern.

Mama, Molly thought. Mary is Mama. What was Daddy talking about? The accident meant something — the secret — was going to be postponed, but what did Mama have to do with it? They hadn't even seen her new dress. They might even have forgotten.

Now three puffed wheats floated, uneaten, in the

pond of sweet milk in Molly's cereal bowl. Molly wished she had a cat, but cats weren't allowed here, only at the feed barns at the mines. "The only earthly place they're any good," Daddy always said.

The sun skitters through the row of Chinese elms that line the road to the mine's feed barn. It is late, but this is summer, and it might be nine o'clock before real darkness closes in.

"Molly," her mother calls, "want a ride?" High up on Ducat's back Molly's mama sits, straight and serene and secure. Mama's saddle for Ducat is different from Daddy's western one, with its horn and fancy flowers worked into the leather of its sides. Mama's is a flat saddle, an English saddle, and Mama's bridle has four reins instead of two and a different, kinder sort of bit for Ducat's mouth than Daddy uses on his quarterhorse. Daddy says the quarterhorse has a hard mouth and is loco besides.

Mama reaches down and pulls Molly up behind her, and as she does she says, "Your daddy thinks he's in the Wild West, honey," and she laughs. "Some little cowboys never do grow up — and your daddy's living proof."

Molly's and Mama's laughter float over the yard, the large open expanse where they exercise the horses on the lunge line and where Molly often rides behind Mama, and sometimes Daddy.

"OK, Ducat, let's go," Mama says, and the huge bay moves out in his easy rack. "He could do this all day, Molly," Mama says.

Molly, too, could do this all day, or even forever. Molly could forever fly through space, high on Ducat's back with the sound of his hooves hitting the earth not coming to her ears but coming in through her lungs, and with Mama here, this safe person to hold on to, and the summer evening, warm and still except for Ducat's hooves and the erratic bursts of activity from Daddy's loco quarterhorse and the sound of the crickets off in the weeds, golden and soft. It is the kind of evening, the kind of summer, that Molly, in her most secret of hearts, wishes would last forever.

7

But it wasn't evening, and this wasn't a dream. It was morning, and Molly ran two at a time upstairs, her seersucker bathrobe flapping out behind her like two big pink cotton wings.

Graham stood in front of Molly's rocking chair, where Molly had put the dress last night, admiring, or at least looking. Not leaving clothes on the rocker was a rule, but Graham agreed that this dress was in a special category.

"Yes indeed," Graham said, "it's perfect. The prettiest dress I've seen in many a year. And sweet little shoes, every bit as pretty, too! You'll be a sight for sore eyes, Miss Molly McAfee."

Graham must know what the surprise is, Molly thought, or else she couldn't say the dress was perfect. Yet Molly couldn't come right out and ask — Graham had probably been sworn to secrecy too.

"I'll put it away," Molly said.

"No, you go on and brush your teeth now," Graham said. "Nobody blames you for wanting to admire your beautiful dress. I'll hang it up for you."

"So you really think it's the right dress, Graham?"

"Yes, indeed, it's just exactly right."

"I mean . . ."

Graham raised one eyebrow and gave Molly a sideways look. Her shrewd eyes were a blue so light they looked right through Molly. Graham smiled, and her tanned leathery cheek turned to a map of well-worn wrinkles. "I know what you're after, Missy. I know your daddy hasn't told you what this dress is for. It's just that the poor man hasn't had the time — that terrible accident and one thing after another. Shame on you, Molly. Trying to trick old Graham."

Molly took great care lacing her sneakers. She didn't look up.

"Now there, honey. I don't blame you. Curiosity's got the best of you, poor little thing."

"Lizzie wouldn't tell me either."

"I know. Be patient, Molly. All in good time."

"But Graham, even if you won't tell me what it is, will you tell me one yes or no? I mean, will you tell me what it isn't, if I guess. What I mean is," and Molly swallowed hard, "is it a wedding? I mean — is Daddy getting married to somebody?"

"Oh, child," Graham said, "what on earth makes you think such a thing? No, no! I can tell you right now, *positively* no."

Graham's assurances sounded definite, certain and strong enough to keep Molly safe from anything.

"Now let's get going, Molly. We all have our work to do today."

Molly got a hanger from the closet, and Graham slipped the white dress onto it, held it out at arm's length, and smiled. "Lizzie said you weren't crazy about your new shoes, but she knows what looks nice. You pay attention to her, you hear, Molly?"

Molly heard, but she didn't hear.

"Molly? Run along now."

Molly studies the linoleum on the kitchen floor beneath her white shoes. It is an extremely complicated pattern. Inlaid, Mama calls it. Molly sits on the low radiator at the end of the kitchen, on top of the flat cover that is the perfect height to sit on. The radiator is so hot that if it weren't for the cover Molly could never sit here. Snow flies past the windows over the kitchen sink.

Daddy doesn't think Molly should sit on the radiator, and she will have to move when he comes back into the room. He has gone to the study to make his journal entries, recording the amounts of cash he has brought home from the mines, and to make out deposit slips so that when he goes to the night depository at the bank, he can just put in the sack of money, and the deposit chute will turn over. The money will be gone, just like magic.

Daddy comes back to the kitchen. "Don't you wish?" he says.

"Mmmm?" Mama says, stirring the gravy.

"Don't you wish we could go somewhere else, do something else? These damned mines," Daddy says.

74

"Oh, Jack," Mama says, "you promised. Your being here means everything to your dad. You said it was settled. Let's not go through that again."

"But," Daddy says, "it's the same. Over and over, day after day." He piles the money up and writes down the total. "I know," he says. "Me and my pipe dreams. But one day, Mary, we're going to take us a trip — a real trip. Around the world! What do you say?"

"I say that sounds wonderful," Mama says.

"Freedom!" Daddy says, and kisses Mama.

Luke peeked through the Mare's fence. On his left hand Luke wore his baseball glove. Obviously Luke had another pitching lesson in mind. In addition, Luke had on his St. Louis Cardinals hat. Grandpa had pitched for the Browns, but Grandpa didn't mind Luke rooting for the Redbirds.

"Luke, come on in," Molly said, even though she knew that was the last thing he would do. Molly was separating a flake of hay for the Mare. Daddy said you always have to do that, or else the horse will eat the hay solid and get a stomachache, and horses sometimes die of indigestion. Horses' digestions can be very delicate, Daddy always warned. Molly wondered if Melissa Tyde knew about pulling apart hay, or if she'd bother to if she did know.

"Where's Grandpa?" Luke said, staying firmly planted outside the fence.

"He and Daddy went to the funeral home. You know about the accident?"

"Yes."

"And you want Grandpa to help you with your pitching, don't you?"

"Yep. Well, if I don't get to throw today, there goes my slider. And just when I almost had it." Luke slapped the wooden fence with his glove. The Mare turned her head at the sound.

"Come in here, so we don't have to yell at each other."

"No, thanks. You think I'm going to let your crazy pony kick me the way the mule did that man?"

"The Mare won't hurt you, Luke. And don't jump to conclusions about Horace. Nobody knows for sure what happened."

"Oh? Just see that look the Mare's giving me. I can tell she doesn't like the way I ride her."

"Actually, Luke, you could be more gentle."

"I wasn't trying to be rough. She just doesn't like me. That's that." Luke slapped the fence with the glove again. Again the Mare's head turned quickly, this time with eyes big and ears flat back. "What'd I tell you? You see that?"

"Oh, Luke, what do you *expect?* You come whacking on her fence with your silly glove. You ought to have sense enough to realize what it sounds like. It sounds exactly like Melissa Tyde's awful crop. Or Daddy and his strap. Horses have memories, too, Luke. Honestly, sometimes you don't use good sense."

"OK, smarty," Luke said, angry. He turned and stalked away toward the house. With every step, he beat the glove against his leg.

Why had Molly said all that? And was Luke being a baby or just not thinking? Besides the Mare, Luke *was* her best friend, like a brother. But Molly couldn't talk to Luke about important things anymore; to Luke the important things had become his slider, baseball cards, and who had the best earned-run average in the National League.

Why couldn't they put their heads together today, for example, and figure out a way to keep the Mare? Or what the secret was? Why couldn't she and Luke agree anymore on the important things? What was so interesting about somebody's batting average, which changed every day, anyway? Why, all of a sudden, did it seem Molly and Luke wanted such different things? Hadn't things always been smooth and easy between them before?

Luke had wandered up to the back lawn, where he tossed his ball up into the trees again, again, again. He wasn't looking Molly's way at all. She had hurt his feelings, and she didn't want Luke mad at her. No matter how silly or childish or selfish he was being.

She finished filling the Mare's trough, patted the pony's neck, and went into the cool, dark garage. She scanned the rafters for something she'd put there a long time ago.

And there it was. On a high nail hung her glove. Molly took a rake handle and lifted it down. Inside, the glove was full of dust. It had been a long time since she and Luke had played catch. The leather was cool and damp, stiff and gritty. Molly worked her fingers into it, opening and closing her hand.

This glove needed saddle soaping and an oiling badly.

"I don't suppose you'd like to play catch," Molly said, squinting as she came back into the sun.

"Well," Luke said, giving it elaborate thought, "you think you can catch me?"

"Really, Luke, you're not all *that* terrific."

Luke threw the ball into his glove three times, each time a little more solidly. He finally grinned. "You're *sure* you're ready for this?"

Molly clinched her teeth and put the glove up, and Luke reared back and threw with all his might.

She blinked. And at the moment her eyes were closed, she heard the plop of the ball in the pocket of her glove and felt a warm sting spreading over the surface of her left palm. "Nice for a slow ball," she said. "Good idea to warm up before you try throwing fast."

Luke put his lower lip out, making a mock pout, and then he smiled again. "Wait till you see my good stuff."

"Oh, dishwater, Luke. This is easy as falling off a log."

The wood floor of the attic is smooth and warm. Molly creeps secretly up the stairs, because Mama doesn't want her to get hurt. The attic is a place full of wonderful old things to discover, but it is dangerous as well. Mama falls once, slips into the place where there's no floor, where the elevator was, and where the motor for the elevator still is. Molly never saw the elevator. Mama had a dream in which Molly learned to walk and then learned to open the metal gate to the elevator, and fell. Grandpa tells the men to leave the hole in the floor, that one day they may change their minds and want the elevator back again.

The pear tree blossoms in one of the windows, fragrant and sweet, and bees hit the screen on the open window all day long. In huge trunks with brass trim and bowed tops, with stickers from everywhere in the world, lay Grandpa's baseball uniforms. Arms and legs folded neatly, with moth-ball dots in every layer. The uniform Grandpa wore the day Daddy was born. The no-hitter uniform. Grandpa's last-game uniform.

At the bottom of the trunks lay nests of base-balls: new ones, old ones, written-up ones covered with teammates from seam to seam.

Bookcases line one side of the attic, and the shelves hold a set of tiny red encyclopedias and old record books from the mines and the scrapbooks.

Molly turns their pages ever so carefully. The old thick sheets crumble in her hands. Here is a picture of Grandpa, looking a little *like Daddy, and even something like Molly.*

Grandpa peers out from young blue eyes, squinting into the photographer's sun. Grandpa with his teammates, half a head taller than anyone else on the team. "You come by your long legs rightly," a voice says from a cloud somewhere else.

8

Molly's long legs dangled from the porch swing, where she and Luke had come to cool off after his thirty pitches. Grandpa told Luke that that was his limit for now. Despite the gloomy morning, the sun finally had made its appearance, and the day had turned just plain hot. But on the front porch you could always find a breeze and a bit of shade. And just as dependably as the shade, Graham would have cold lemonade, sweet as summer itself.

They rested and drank. "Too bad you're not a boy," Luke finally said.

That exact thought had never occurred to Molly. She had wondered what it was like being a boy, but not that she would rather be one. Why should such a thing occur to Luke? That sounded like something Luke was repeating, something he'd heard.

"I don't know about that," Molly said. "Why?"

"You're so by yourself here — just you, the only

girl, with your daddy and your grandpa. Doesn't being the only girl get lonely?"

"We still have each other for best friends, don't we?" Molly said.

Luke looked up. Best friends with a girl? He had caught a grasshopper, and he stroked its antennae. "Sure, Molly."

"I have a problem, Luke. I have to figure out some way to get rid of Melissa Tyde."

"You mean, bump her off?"

"No, silly. I mean just discourage her from wanting the Mare. Any normal person would have had enough, getting thrown that way, but not Melissa. I just have a terrible feeling that she would be mean to the Mare."

"What does she want with a pony in the first place?" Luke asked.

"That's part of the problem. I'm not sure, exactly. Dr. Tyde —"

"Ugggh, Dr. Tyde! Just his name gives me the creeps —"

"Come on, Luke, listen. The more I think of it, I'm sure that it's not so much Melissa as Dr. Tyde. He keeps talking about what a terrific rider he was himself. I think Melissa's trying to impress her daddy."

"Weird," said Luke.

"Yes. Weird is right."

"I don't know, Molly. I don't have any ideas. It seems pretty complicated to me."

"I guess it's hopeless, trying to change the Tydes'

minds. There's no way I can deal with the two of them. What I've got to do is come up with some plan — something to take away Daddy's reasons for selling the Mare."

"But what?" Luke said.

"That's the problem. *What?*" Molly shook her head.

Luke ducked his head and his grasshopper spit out some tobacco juice, just like Grandpa, who regularly chewed his "t'baccy," just like when he played ball. "Yuck," said Luke, wiping his hand on his pants. "You ever try Grandpa's chewing tobacco?"

"Loose or plug?"

"Either one."

"I tried the loose. You want to feel sick at your stomach, just try chewing tobacco."

"Maybe the plug's better," Luke said.

"No, Daddy said it's stronger. I don't see how it could be. It's really disgusting stuff."

"Grandpa likes it."

"It's a habit, he says."

"I wonder if I have to chew to be a pitcher."

"Why would you? That doesn't necessarily have to be, Luke. Lots of people chew tobacco who never played baseball. Why shouldn't it work the other way around?"

"Maybe you're right. You know where Grandpa keeps his tobacco?"

"No, Molly lied. She knew, of course, exactly where it was: the top right-hand drawer of his desk, the little narrow drawer that had the inkwell hole in it and a tray where Grandpa kept the ivory-handled knife he used to slice off the plug tobacco, between his thumb and the knife. It made Molly nervous to watch how he'd slip the tobacco sliver into his mouth, without even closing the blade. She wasn't about to tell Luke where the tobacco was. He'd get sick at his stomach, she knew it, and then Grandpa would guess what had happened.

Luke threw the grasshopper out into the air. Like magic, it grew wings and sailed over the porch rail into the bushes.

Molly felt restless. "If you're through with your lemonade, Luke," she said, "I'll take your glass inside."

Luke handed her the glass, but he stayed on the swing and gave it a push with his feet. "I'm going to wait here for Grandpa and think," Luke said. "Maybe I'll get an idea."

"Fine," Molly said, and then she couldn't resist. She gave Luke's burr a gentle rub and said, "This'll be a first." And then she hurried in the front door. She would go through the house, out back, and curry the Mare.

"Here's how you do it, Molly-o," Mama says. "You go backward with the currycomb, against the way the fur lies. Then you go in circles, just like the currycomb itself."

Molly doesn't want to be here. Luke and Lizzie have gone to the school picnic right after the parade, but Mama has made Molly come with her. By now Luke is riding the Tilt-a-Whirl or the Ferris wheel or the Flying Swings, or he's eating pink cotton candy and drinking his third red soda pop and eating hot dogs and popcorn. Luke's mother, though, didn't lead the parade on her horse, the way Molly's did, and so Luke's mother doesn't have to take care of a horse.

Molly doesn't want to be here. She would rather be at the school picnic. By the time she and Mama get there, it will be half over.

Molly holds the silly currycomb up to the light, looking through its nest of three metal circles with their jagged edges. She frowns.

"Don't worry about hurting Ducat, Molly," Mama says. "His skin is tough. He loves having his back scratched."

Ducat lifts his rear hoof. Is he going to kick? He sets his hoof back down with a clunk.

"He's just swishing flies," Mama says. "Horses do that, even if there's not a fly for miles around. I sometimes think a horse does that just to keep from getting bored."

Ducat stands in the afternoon shade. His head lolls lazily. From time to time, he swishes his tail. He sends out one of those wonderful, strange shivers that horses can do: moving the skin on their legs or their withers, or shaking their manes without moving their heads. Ducat flicks just one ear. Molly doesn't see any horseflies, or any other kind of flies either. Mama must be right: Ducat is just occupying himself.

84

"*I know you'd rather be at the school picnic, Molly, but when there's a job to do, you have to do it. Self-discipline gives you inner resources,*" *Mama says to Molly, smiling.* "*Look at old Ducat — just think the tales he could tell us if only he could talk!*"

Mama crouches down to brush the mud from Ducat's hooves. Her face is level with Molly's.

But the picnic.

"*Little girls, too,*" *Mama says. Her voice is gentle, like a song on the wind.* "*Little girls need to do things when they should be done — that's self-discipline. Otherwise you can't do your work, and think for yourself and solve your problems, and follow your thoughts through. Those are inner resources.*"

Molly's not sure she understands exactly what Mama's talking about, but she will remember it, just in case.

Mama has Ducat's hooves all clean, brushed to a shoe-polish shine with the stiff brown-bristled brush.

"*Foot-cleaning time, Mr. Ducat.*" *Ducat looks around. Mama takes the hoof knife from her back pocket and opens it up. She scrapes the dirt away from Ducat's shoe and from the frog, inside his hoof.* "*Easy, there — such a big baby,*" *she says to the horse.* "*You have to keep your horse's hooves clean, Molly, or he'll turn up lame.*"

Mama finishes at last. Ducat's coat gleams like a piece of beautiful wood, and Mama feeds him.

They can go now to the school picnic. Their work is finished.

Behind them, Molly hears Ducat's big round teeth chewing. The lock on the stable door clicks.

In the Mare's little stable, the crickets clicked and sang. The Mare dozed in the shady space of her stall, with a narrow ribbon of sunshine strung from the stable door to her left rear hoof.

While she made circles with the currycomb, Molly thought about this morning. Grandpa had been on the phone with his lawyer, talking about "the plans" and about something that had been "Mary's and Jack's" and that "I think Jack should go ahead and give it anyway." The secret.

Who was Daddy giving something to, and what was it?

To Molly?

Something in place of the Mare? Or did it have nothing to do with Molly, except that she needed a new dress? Why couldn't they just tell her? Why were they so busy all the time?

Molly pulled the Mare's loose fur out of the currycomb, hung it on its hook, and began brushing the Mare's fur smooth. Taking care of a pony wasn't particularly fun, but Molly didn't mind the work if it was for the Mare. How many times would Melissa Tyde curry a pony? Twice, maybe? Molly had to convince Daddy she should keep the Mare. Anything, just so Melissa got over wanting to buy her. Molly wondered how much Melissa really even liked horses.

And poor Horace.

By now they had probably brought him up out of the mine, everyone with an eagle eye on him, the way they do with mad dogs, to see if he acts crazy and tries to hurt someone else. *If* he actually hurt Mr. Haller. Molly didn't believe it. Would Daddy have news about Horace when he came home for dinner?

"Hi, Molly, honey," a voice said.

"Aunt Lizzie, you're back!"

"Me and my brand-new filling. Just one, thank heaven. Where's Luke? I didn't realize how late it was."

"He's on the porch, thinking," Molly said. "He's been waiting for Grandpa. I guess I'm not much of a battery mate."

"Say, which club's this?" Daddy asked, popping his head in at the stable door. "You didn't even see me follow you right in the drive, Liz."

"Oh, my mind's a million miles away, Jack. How did it go?"

"Not so well. Why don't you come up to the house for a minute. I'd like to talk if you're not in a rush."

"Of course," Lizzie said. Then she added, "Molly, sweetheart, will you ask Luke to get his things together — we'll be leaving in a bit."

Already talking, a shell around them the way grown-ups sometimes have, Daddy and Lizzie walked away.

9

Everywhere, everywhere, there are flowers.

Flowers sprout from the floor and from the walls; they hang from the ceiling. They float everywhere in the thick, heavy perfume smell they are making. The room is large, but it is too small. There is no air. There are far too many people to fit here, too many to all come in and greet and stand, sighing, looking, for a few minutes.

Everyone is here to look at Mama and all her flowers.

They call it visitation hours. People come to pay their last respects. Molly thinks the words don't exactly fit. She thinks it would be a lot more respectful if everyone would just go away. Molly doesn't want to be here, collecting people's last respects, writing it all down, like Daddy writing in his journal from the mine, making the deposit in the night depository. For what?

Molly would rather be anyplace else in the

world just now, even, she thinks, at the bottom of the Mississippi.

Molly closes her eyes.

Fishes and eels and mud puppies and frogs swim every which way with the snakes and animals so small no one can see them as they drift past. The water is milky brown. It moves like a thick wind in swirls around Molly's head, pulling her clothes out away from her in round pillows, this way and that, and rushing past with a low, steady roar that is so constant it is at first not even noticeable. Molly feels her feet sink into the sand and mud bottom. She braces her feet to withstand the current and realizes the mud-sand is warmer than the water. Waterlogged pieces of wood, no longer able to float, rush past Molly's eyes in the fast current. Molly knows she must open her eyes now. She must breathe.

She opens her eyes, and everyone is still here, all over everything, everywhere. People. Fish faces. Their mouths open and close, their eyes blink, bubbles of sound come out. All are saying exactly the same words. Sometimes the words are slightly rearranged, but they are the same. Everyone feels the same: everyone loves Mama. Such a kind a wonderful a beautiful a generous lady, such a shame a shame a shame, how terrible dreadful awful tragic.

Yes, yes, Molly knows, she nods. She knows there was no one like her mother, not anywhere in the whole world, and now not even that. And Molly has something to say to Mama, something to talk about, but now Mama can't hear her. The beautiful lady in the box isn't talking and can't hear, doesn't look real and probably isn't even Mama at all. It's some wax doll.

But Molly isn't fooled by this wax figure. She has looked at the doll-Mama once, and that is all she will do. There hadn't been any way to avoid it. Daddy is there, touching Mama's stiff, dry hair. It's not Mama's hair, that does what it wants to because it is curly, like Molly's. Grandpa is blowing his nose very loudly. Mama would have a fit if she heard that. That was something that Mama really insisted on — you had to blow your nose quietly.

People still are coming and coming and the room seems it will burst, it is so full of flowers and people and words. Black clothes sift in and out. The scene makes Molly think of picture negatives — with Mama's opposite white wedding dress, at the other end of everything. Now it is late and time to go home. But more people come, and still people are outside when finally Grandpa tells Daddy that he will take Molly home. "Half of Comfort is here tonight," Grandpa tells Daddy, and Daddy's face is wet with tears.

Molly knows all the people are saying how much they loved her mother. But they don't know how much Molly loved her, and how much Molly needed Mama to come back.

Mama, Molly said inside herself all those many nights, and all those many days. Mama?

Daddy had stopped the car in front of Whitelaw's Funeral Home.

Molly had never liked Daddy's car, maybe because it had only two doors. Or maybe because she usually had to sit in the back. It was hard to get out. The seats were itchy wool, besides.

Grandpa drew a deep breath. "Well, Jack, no use postponing the inevitable," he said.

"You're right, Pa. Let's go in," Daddy said, taking out the key and opening his door.

Grandpa got out too and held his seat forward so Molly could climb out.

"Molly, you don't have to stay long if you don't want to," Daddy said. "Say hello to Mrs. Haller and the children, and say something extra to Elaine. It will be all right if you come back outside. They will understand."

"All right," Molly said.

"Where are all the other people?" Molly asked Daddy in the vestibule.

He shook his head, put his finger up to his lips, and only said, "It's early." Why were only two cars standing in the parking lot? Had Daddy made a mistake and come to the wrong funeral home? Had the doctors made a mistake, and Mr. Haller had recovered, after all?

No. That was foolishness. If Grandpa could read minds, he would be angry.

In the hallway stood a little easel. On its black grooved board in little white letters was the name

HALLER. There was no mistake. It had all happened; it was real, all right.

Parlor C.

Molly remembered this place. This hallway, so quiet, so empty. Now there were no flowers here.

Parlor C was the last room and the smallest. Two table lamps cast a rosy light, and next to one of them, in a wing chair that sat near the head of the casket, sat Mrs. Haller, whose eyes looked black and tired. She got up when she saw the McAfees come into the room. Molly saw right away that Mrs. Haller was pregnant. Very pregnant.

"Mr. McAfee," she said, taking Grandpa's hand. Her eyes glistened. "Mr. Jack. Thank you both for coming."

Daddy and Grandpa said all the usual things. Sorry. A real tragedy, a shame. A terrible, sad accident. What could they do?

"At the moment, I can't think what," Mrs. Haller said. "But I must thank you for the beautiful flowers, the roses from the company and the basket from you, Mr. McAfee. They're right in front. Beautiful, aren't they?"

Molly hung behind Daddy and Grandpa, shifting around, pretending to look at the flowers, but really trying to stay out of Mrs. Haller's line of sight.

"His father's coming in tonight, Mr. Jack," Mrs. Haller was saying. "The train from Little Rock gets to St. Louis at nine-thirty."

"That will help you, Martha, being together as a family. His mother's coming, too, I take it?"

"Yes, she's coming. This has hit her pretty hard.

You know, I worry about Bert's ma. She takes on about things."

"Of course," Daddy said.

"Perhaps I'll be wrong," Mrs. Haller said. "I hope so. She's not likely to be much of a comfort, and the children are already confused. I just don't know how I'll manage . . ."

"Let me at least go pick up Albert's folks at the train for you," Grandpa said.

"Oh, that would put you to too much trouble, Mr. McAfee. I couldn't ask you to do that."

"Nonsense," Grandpa said. "You didn't ask — I offered. Well, that settles that."

Mrs. Haller's face relaxed a bit. "That'll mean a lot to me, Mr. McAfee. Thank you." She turned around and looked at the row of four children sitting evenly spaced on the long blue camelback sofa against the parlor wall. "Come, children, and meet the McAfees. This is your young one, Mr. Jack?"

"Yes," Daddy said, sounding distracted, "I'm sorry. This is Molly, my daughter."

Molly shook hands and said to Mrs. Haller, "How do you do?" That was a dumb, stupid question. Why should Mrs. Haller be doing anything but terrible? "I was very sorry to hear about the accident, Mrs. Haller."

"Thank you, Molly. Elaine tells me you're in the same grade at school?"

"Yes, that's right. Elaine, I'm sorry to hear about your father." Elaine shook Molly's hand stiffly. It was a hot evening, but Elaine's hand was ice cold.

As Molly looked at Elaine Haller for an extra moment, she finally grasped why she never knew Elaine at school. Elaine looked just the same as always, except dressed up, but she was the kind of person no one paid any attention to: everything about her blended into the background. She walked as if she were tired, with her head down and with her back curved the wrong way — the way Mama wouldn't let Molly stand. Elaine's light brown hair, standing out with electricity from brushing, was pinned with silvery barrettes above each of her ears.

Molly felt sad. Elaine was trying to look her best. She was just a plain girl, with a plain face and plain hair. Elaine never seemed to have any life or pep, and now she had even less. Molly thought, all at once, of Melissa Tyde — how pretty she was, how opposite in every way. At school, Elaine wasn't bad, or disliked. She was someone that just didn't seem to count.

Daddy and Mrs. Haller were talking. Molly said something to Elaine about the flowers, just to be talking too. Empty words.

Actually, Elaine's pale blue dress was what made Molly feel like crying: it must have belonged to someone else. It was too big for Elaine. Molly could tell it wasn't new because it had that dusty look that cotton dresses get when they have been washed and ironed a lot. The huge dress had been starched, and it stood out and up from Elaine's shoulders like a piece of metal armor, a shape that had nothing to do with the body inside. The cotton skirt was very, very long and very full. Elaine's bare ankles were pale.

Her eyes were red, but she wasn't crying.

Finally Molly heard herself say, "Elaine, would you like to come outside? I saw a nice place to sit — a bench out in the garden."

Elaine turned to her mother. "Mom? All right?"

"Yes, sure, Elaine. That's a good idea. You take Billy and Karl with you."

Elaine and Molly walked side by side down the hall. Elaine's two little brothers rushed ahead, out the door into the dusk, giggling. The little boys didn't understand, Molly realized. She bet Elaine wished she didn't understand either. Understanding only went so far.

Molly couldn't tell Elaine how much she wished she weren't here, or what she thought about Horace and the so-called accident. It wasn't Horace's fault and he couldn't even defend himself. What did Mrs. Haller expect them to do with Horace. Treat him like a rabid dog? "Execute" — that's what they would do to him. There were times when you just couldn't say what you thought. This was one of them.

Molly was glad she held her tongue because Elaine sniffed and pulled a tissue out of a pocket in her full skirt. She unfolded the tissue and stared at it as though the secret to life were written on it. "Are you having a nice summer, Molly?"

"Yes, I suppose so," Molly said, ashamed. What if

Elaine asked her what she'd been doing? Would she make something up, to not make Elaine feel worse? She could never tell Elaine the truth about the kind of summer she was having. It wouldn't make any sense to Elaine, especially not here and now. How would it help Elaine? The truth and the whole truth wouldn't help anybody.

Molly sits on the judge's bench wearing a white curly wig, a black robe. In her hand she holds a gavel, which she brings to the block on the desk with a resounding bang.

"The defendant will rise," a voice says.

Horace, in the witness box, stands at attention. His huge ears are forward, alert.

"The Court has a few questions for the Defendant," Molly says. Her voice is unusually stern. "First, what is your complete name?"

Horace stands, his big brown eyes studying Molly inquisitively. He says nothing.

"The Defendant is instructed to answer the Court's question," Molly directs.

Horace swishes his tail and flicks his ears, first one, then the other. Still he does not answer.

"You are being uncooperative," Molly says irritably. "Even if you are a mule, don't be a mule."

Horace blows air out of his nostrils, a big, noisy snuffle.

"And don't be rude. Even mules must use their handkerchiefs. You'll have to mind your manners in my courtroom," Molly says, "and while you're at it, watch your posture."

*Out of nowhere Elaine materializes and ap-
proaches the bench.*

*"Your Honor," she addresses Molly, "the Prose-
cution moves that the record show that we have
here an uncooperative Defendant. The Prosecution begs that the Court cite this Defendant for
contempt."*

*What has come over Elaine? Molly wonders.
Dull, uninteresting, know-nothing Elaine — the
attorney for the prosecution? Where did she get
that briefcase and all those words, and why is she
wearing her father's good blue serge suit?*

*"Motion denied," Molly says. She cracks the
gavel sharply on the block. "The Defendant is
hereby sentenced to learn to talk within the next
forty-eight hours, or show cause why final sen-
tence should not be passed."*

*Horace blinks and Molly wants to cry, and she
hopes that this is a dream, because talking, for
Horace, is simply out of the question.*

"Billy? Karl? Where are you?"

Elaine stretched up on her toes to look out over
the hedge. "Where could they have gone to?" she
asked Molly with worry in her voice.

"I can't imagine," Molly said. How could the
boys have slipped away in the few minutes she and
Elaine were talking. "Shall I look inside and see if
they're there?"

"Yes. I'll look in the parking lot, and around the
back of the building. Just don't let Mom find out I
let them wander off."

97

"Oh, no — don't worry," Molly said. She hurried up the funeral home's front steps, through the double doors, and down the hall. In Parlor C, three more men and two women had joined Grandpa and Daddy and Mrs. Haller. They were all seated in a kind of circle, the chairs pulled up, talking quietly together. Only the youngest Haller child, who had stayed inside with her mother, was in the room, playing with a truck on a string. Molly ducked away from the door so no one would catch a glimpse of her.

"Bil-ly? Ka-rl?" Elaine came through the porte-cochère where the endless black Cadillac hearse was parked. It had black curtains faded to navy blue that were pulled back with black silk rosettes, just the way little kids draw windows with smiley curtains in their kindergarten houses. Elaine glanced sideways, into the hearse, and Molly's heart hurt.

"They weren't inside? Where can they be?" Elaine was crying.

"Elaine, please. Just stop for a second. Relax. They've got to be here somewhere. Let me go out on the sidewalk and see if they're out there." But there were no little boys on the sidewalk, in the street, across the street, anywhere. "We'll find them, Elaine," Molly told her. You must keep a cool head, Molly told herself.

"Let's just sit down where we were," Molly said, "and figure this out calmly. Maybe we can hear them," she said. They listened, but at first all they could hear was the locusts singing their every-evening song in the high old trees.

Then they looked at each other. Another sound

98

was mixed in with the cicadas' drone — a steady scratching noise from the midst of a thick clump of weigela bushes. Without a word, Molly and Elaine crept toward the shrubs.

"I'm digging to China," Billy said.

"No, you're not," Karl said.

"Yes, I am."

"I'm older, and I ought to know," Karl told him.

"All right, then, if I'm not digging to China, I'm getting coal."

"No, you're not."

"Yes, I am. Just like Daddy."

"Bill, there is no more Daddy," Karl said. "Daddy died."

"All right, then," Billy said. "I know what I'm doing. I'm making the hole to put him in."

Elaine drew in a breath. Molly was afraid to look at her. At least five years' time had helped Molly with the pain of losing Mama. At least Molly had the Mare to make her think of something else. At least Molly knew she would have a safe home, enough to eat, and more than she needed or wanted to wear.

Molly put her arm around Elaine. How alike but different they were. Molly's head was spinning with memories and the years since Mama died, that big gaping hole where she and Mama never got to set things right.

For Elaine the hurt was all right here, and it was all right now.

IO

    Any minute Graham would bustle in to shake Molly out of her dreams — Molly could count on that every morning.

But today would not be like every other day. It would not be a day like *any* other day. At 2:30 this afternoon Mr. Haller's funeral would take place. Today would not be like some other summer day when she and Luke might amuse themselves with a difference of opinion, or when she and Grandpa might have a lazy summer talk about everything-in-general-and-nothing-in-particular out under the elms, the traffic going by every now and then to nowhere special.

Last night Molly tried staying awake, lying in bed, to hear Grandpa get home, but it didn't work. The Hallers' train from Arkansas must have come in very late.

"Morning, sweet pea." Graham's head popped through Molly's doorway. "Time to rise and shine."

Molly quickly closed her eyes. Maybe Graham hadn't seen her looking up at the ceiling. No, too late.

"Now don't you try playing possum on me, Miss Molly. I'm on to your tricks. The day's not going to go away, no matter how long you stay in bed."

"I know," Molly said. "Today's the funeral, whether I stay in bed or not. I don't want to go but maybe it would help Elaine if I went. We had never talked before last night. She's nice. A hundred times nicer than that awful Melissa Tyde, that much is sure!"

"Molly McAfee, you're as transparent as a pane of glass, I declare. You don't want that Melissa to have your pony. Though I will say she's not the kind I'd want to have my pony either." Graham opened the curtains.

The light streamed into Molly's bedroom, and she put the pillow over her head.

"I'm glad you and Elaine got acquainted," Graham went on. "Poor little thing. Well, no use delaying the inevitable." Graham tossed Molly a clean pair of blue jeans and a red gingham shirt from the dresser. "You have to go on as if it were any other day, say good morning to the Mare, go about your chores as usual. Let's go, Molly. You're keeping your daddy and grandpa waiting."

Molly-in-the-mirror didn't have combed hair and couldn't stop for that. Grandpa predicted Molly would break her neck on the stairs one day, but she still took them two at a time going down. From the kitchen came the smell of oranges and toast and coffee and bacon, and the sound of Daddy and Grandpa talking.

"So, Pa, you think she plans to sue the company, then?" Daddy said.

Molly stopped dead in her tracks. She stayed around the corner just outside the kitchen door, listening in the dining room.

"Good heaven, Jack, I don't know. Nothing would surprise me after the way old Al's wife carried on. That woman was in one terrible state last night. You've never seen anyone go on so, and in a public place. It was almost more than old Al and I could do to control her."

She? Her? There were two Mrs. Hallers. Elaine's mother and her grandmother. The *she* who might sue was Elaine's mother.

"Molly ought to be up and stirring by now," Daddy said. "Molly!"

Molly retraced her steps soundlessly back around the dining room table and hurried into the kitchen. "Hi, Daddy — hi, Grandpa."

"Graham's squeezed your nice fresh orange juice, Molly, and look here, your favorite," Grandpa said, lifting the cover on the plate. "Bacon, just the way you like it. Now make yourself some toast and have a bacon sandwich."

Molly put the bread in the toaster and pushed the handle down.

"Come here, Molly," Daddy said, gathering her into a rough hug. "You know, I think you can just stay home today. You don't need to go to the funeral."

"Are you sure?"

"I don't think it's such a good idea, honey," Grandpa said after a moment. "And nobody really expects it of you."

"But what about Elaine? She might expect me to come, and I'm not afraid to go," Molly said, just so they knew.

"Sweetheart, we know. But you went with us last night, and we think it will be better this way," Daddy said.

"Molly, all the men from the mine who worked with Mr. Haller will be there today. Plenty of folks will be around, if that's what's bothering you. It won't be empty like last night."

"Are you sure? Maybe you should tell Elaine I don't feel well. To tell you the truth, I really don't."

"All right, we'll tell her. Not a summer cold, is it?" Grandpa asked, like a doctor.

"No, I didn't sleep much last night. Maybe I can take a nap. Maybe I'll clean the Mare's tack — in case we sell her — and I have some thinking to do. Graham and I'll keep each other company."

MCAFEE COAL COMPANY, the mine stationery says. It is in a drawer in Grandpa's desk, a peculiar drawer that has slanted slots in it for different kinds of paper.

Everybody in Comfort knows the McAfee Coal Company or has someone in his family or knows somebody who has worked at some point, in some capacity, for the McAfee Coal Company. At the very least, they all buy their coal from the Mc-Afees. The big maroon trucks are all over Comfort in the wintertime, though right now most of them sit still and quiet in the machinery building, resting for the summer. The trucks are monsters, Molly thinks, with tires that were, for a long time, bigger than she. The tires have thick V's going round them, one after another, like huge black rubber birds.

Luke thinks the coal dump trucks are so wonderful! To Molly their size and noise are frightening and terrible. Winters, she watches as they bring coal to her house. She watches as the driver raises the truck higher and the coal falls out through the little door at the back. The coal rushes all at once to the door and falls down the chute into the coal bin, like a lake of black water rushing toward the whirlpool where it drains out. The noise is a million pieces of coal, Molly thinks, all making clicks and tiny crashes, blending into a kind of constant hiss. The black mountain grows, glinting in the half-light that sneaks in the chute door.

Then the coal is all down and the truck is empty, and the driver lets the truck bed down. So slowly it falls, more slowly than Molly ever dreamed.

In the beginning, Molly hoped that someday she and the Mare would win a ribbon, but she never dreamed of so many. Molly opened the door of the closet that Daddy called — with a smile — Molly's Tack Room, and ribbons in every color fluttered hello. Today was a perfect day for cleaning tack: you could think while you cleaned tack, and Molly needed to think.

Molly looped her arm through the Mare's bridle, rummaged for the saddle soap and sponges and rags, and lifted the saddle off its rack. Oil and leather and soap — Molly liked the smell of the tack room. The three serious silver trophies were in the house; Molly liked the happy ribbons better, and the Mare could enjoy them too. Did Melissa understand that trophies weren't won without first winning ribbons?

From the spigot next to the Mare's stall door, Molly filled a small can of water. She sat down on a bale of hay and put the saddle over one of her legs.

She twisted the lid off the saddle soap tin, and wet the tan shell of soap that showed the metal through at the bottom. The soap foamed up merrily. Molly hummed and transferred the soapy suds to the saddle's flaps.

CASTLEBERRY'S HARNESS CLEANSER, the tin read. Molly turned the lid around, right side up, so she could read the rest, including the fine print. She hummed and scrubbed, scrubbed and hummed, rubbing the saddle in circles. Humming while she worked was a habit — it didn't necessarily mean she was happy. Now, how unimportant the dress-surprise had become. Molly had more serious problems to think about, and she was worried. About the funeral, about Melissa Tyde and the Mare. About Elaine and her family, who might be suing the McAfee Coal Company. About poor Horace, gentle Horace, who couldn't defend himself.

"Why fret about things you can't help?" Grandpa always said. Which things could Molly really do something about? Which were most important? And which were things that no amount of thinking would change?

Molly would know about the funeral soon, and if Elaine really wanted Molly for a friend, it would happen. Maybe Elaine would never want to speak to her again if things got ugly, people suing each other and all.

And the Mare?

There was a problem Molly might be able to do something about. Though it wasn't going to be easy.

What on earth would keep Daddy from selling the Mare? Whether the Mare was sold to that Miss Priss Melissa or not — that wasn't so important.

No, what had made Daddy want to sell the Mare?

To be mean to Molly? No.

To get the money? No.

To clear out the back field for something else? No.

Then why?

It was simple. The Mare was just too little for Molly to ride. Nothing could change that. Molly just wasn't petite, like Melissa, and she couldn't shrink, couldn't be seven again.

And why did it bother Daddy so? Because the Mare wasn't getting exercise. She was just vegetating in her pasture.

"This fine emollient cleanser is unsurpassed for the care of saddles, harnesses, and all leather goods," said the saddle soap.

Molly blinked.

She read the tin again.

Saddles, harnesses, all leather goods. The words had a hypnotic rhythm.

At the door of the tiny stable Graham appeared, breaking into Molly's daydream. "I'm going to walk up to the corner, Molly," she said. "How I managed to run clean out of bluing, I don't know. But I've got two loads of white wash that can't wait."

"I'll go for you, Graham. What brand — La France?"

"No, that's all right, sugar. I see you're right busy yourself. I'll just be a minute, and I love the fresh air."

"All right, if you're sure," Molly said. "I've got plenty to do here." Graham tucked her big black seal pocketbook under her thick tanned arm and strode off. Graham walked as though she could walk forever. Molly thought maybe she could. When she was a little girl, Graham told Molly, she walked seven miles a day to and from her one-room school in Carolina.

Saddles, harnesses, all leather goods.

The words echoed in Molly's head, and with the echo came an idea.

A way to save the Mare.

It was so simple that Molly wondered how she hadn't thought of it before: the one perfect way to convince Daddy that she should keep the Mare, forever. She hoped she could make it work.

One problem solved, Molly thought. She smiled and buffed the saddle flap dry and shiny, and worked the rag through the leather keeper. Such a still morning! No wind stirring the trees, and Central Avenue with not the least bit of traffic. Molly could hear every bird's song. She could even hear the telephone ringing, way up in the house.

Oh! *Molly* had to answer it. She pushed the saddle off her knee and ran for the back door. By the time she reached the phone, she was completely out of breath. "Hello?" she said, panting. "McAfees' residence."

"I know who it is," a voice said.

"What?" Molly said, thinking she hadn't heard right.

"I said, I know very well who it is."

"Who is *this?*" Molly asked.

"This is the Voice of Truth," the person on the phone said.

"What?"

"This is the Voice of Truth," it repeated slowly, "and I will not be stilled."

Molly hung up the phone.

Instantly, it started ringing again.

Molly just let it.

It wouldn't stop.

"Leave me alone, whoever you are!" Molly said when she picked up the phone.

"Molly!" her grandfather's voice said, "what on earth's wrong with you?"

"Oh, Grandpa, it's just you!" How could she tell him about the crazy phone call? Grandpa had enough problems. "Oh, that silly Luke's always playing games with the phone." But Molly knew it hadn't been Luke. It was a grown-up woman's voice.

"In a pig's eye, Molly. Now what's going on there? I want the truth!"

"Nothing, really Grandpa. I guess it *must* have been Luke, playing some kind of joke."

"I don't want to hear tell of you answering the phone like that again, young lady. *That* was terrible."

"I won't Grandpa. I'm sorry."

"All right, then. Now will you please be sure to tell Graham that we won't be home until a little after five. We'll see you then."

"All right, Grandpa."

Molly hung up the phone.

"Who's that?" Graham said behind her, and Molly nearly jumped out of her skin.

II

∂ "What's going on here, Molly? Who was on the phone?" Graham asked again. "And what's come over you, jumping like a scared rabbit?"

"You startled me," Molly said. Would Graham's sixth sense tell her what had really happened? "It was only Grandpa. He just wanted to say he and Daddy will be home around five." Molly didn't plan to tell Graham about hearing from the Voice of Truth.

"That's just like Mr. Rob, so considerate, with all he's got on his mind, poor man."

Could Grandpa's mind, or Daddy's be any fuller than Molly's? Whatever problems they had, she had. Plus Melissa. Plus whatever it was they weren't getting around to telling her. It seemed only fair: if they could have their secret, Molly could have hers, and hers would be the Voice of Truth.

Graham said her small mountain of wash was waiting. Molly told Graham she wanted to get a book in the living room, but what she really wanted was to be close to the phone. Just in case.

Somehow she just knew the Voice of Truth would try to call back. It hadn't finished saying all it meant to — she had hung up on it. And probably made it mad. But when would the call come? Molly would wait.

She opened the glass door of Mama's bookcase. Mama had had the two cases built, one on either side of the fireplace. One was for Mama's literature books, the other held Daddy's engineering books and Grandpa's old medical books. The engineering books Molly couldn't read — they were what Mama called "higher mathematics," full of letters and numbers Molly never saw anywhere else. Molly liked the medical books and being able to see inside people.

But Mama's books were the ones Molly loved best because they were made out of people's imaginations for other people's imaginations. There were big books of Chaucer and Milton and Shakespeare and Alexander Pope, which Mama told Molly she might not understand right away, but one day she would. There was Wordsworth and Shelley and Browning; Mama had lots of poetry books in Italian and French and Balzac's novels, and novels by Dickens and Thackeray and Jane Austen and the Brontës.

Molly loved to hold the books and imagine the magic worlds the words on the pages made. She pulled her favorite, *Wuthering Heights*, out, and it fell open to her place from last summer, marked with a robin's plantain, thin and dry as if Graham had ironed it. The moors of England, such a magic, sad place, Molly thought wistfully. But reading about Heathcliff and Cathy today wasn't as magic as last time. Maybe it wasn't Emily Brontë's fault.

Molly knew it was the Voice of Truth, out there somewhere, getting ready to call.

Molly's number is 321. Some people in Comfort have four numbers, and some — the people on party lines — have four numbers with a letter after it, like 4579-J. In St. Louis, where phones have dials, they have a word and five numbers. How can anyone remember all that? The people in St. Louis must have to use those big fat phone books all the time.

The Comfort phone book is thin and light because Comfort is a very small town. Everyone in Comfort knows exactly where the phone company is, downtown on Illinois Avenue. Molly has never been inside it, but she can imagine the phone company in full detail. Next year in seventh grade they will take a field trip to the phone company, but for now, Molly's made-up picture is just fine. She sees rows of operators with complicated boards of holes in front of them and little wires with plugs that go from one hole to another, each for a different phone number — just like in the movies. Molly's is an easy number; the McAfees have always had that number, from the very first, Grandpa tells her.

The phone is ringing. Molly answers it.

"I am a friend," says the voice.

"Oh, that's nice," Molly says. "What's your name?"

"That's not important," the friend says. "Are you the little girl with the pony?"

"That's right, I'm Molly," she says. "I just got the pony. It was my birthday present, and everybody at the party rode it and had a wonderful time."

"I know," the friend says. Molly thinks yes, this must be a friend, but who?

"You're not taking good care of your pony," the friend says.

"Oh yes, I am."

"No, you're not. I walked by your house last night, by your pony's pasture. I saw him standing there in the rain."

"It's a her. It's a mare."

"It doesn't matter," says the friend. "You should take better care of your pony. If you don't, one day you might not have it."

"You don't understand — the Mare likes the rain. This is Indian summer. The rain doesn't hurt her. It's good for her."

"No, it's not. She doesn't like it, I can tell. One day she might just run away."

"No, she wouldn't do that. She can get into her stall anytime she wants. Horses like to stand in the summer rain sometimes. That's what my mama used to say."

"Who cares what your mama said? Just don't be

so sure that nothing's going to happen to your precious pony." The voice doesn't sound like a friend now.

"I won't let anything happen to her," Molly says. Her voice sounds higher, tighter. She may cry.

"Yes, indeed, that certainly would be terrible," the voice says. Then it laughs a strange laugh. "A regular shame."

"I have to go now," Molly says. She doesn't like this person who laughs about terrible things.

"What's the matter? Don't you like talking to your friends?"

"Yes," Molly says. "It's been nice talking to you. Good-bye."

She hangs up the phone. She wants to pick the phone up again and ask the operator for 654, please, which is the Coal Company office. Not to tell on the friend who called, but just to talk with Grandpa or Daddy, someone safe.

Before she does, the phone rings again.

Quickly Molly put the robin's plantain marker back in *Wuthering Heights*, and ran to the phone. "Hello?" she said.

"Hello," the voice said. "I expect you know who this is."

"No, I don't," Molly said. She didn't, but she did know it was the Voice of Truth agian.

"It's Truth," said the voice.

Molly said nothing.

"Are you still there?" the voice wanted to know.

"Yes, I'm still here."

"Well, Miss Molly McAfee, you listen to me, and listen good."

"I'm listening."

"You McAfees think you can run things any way you like in Comfort. You think because those hell-hole coal mines give people jobs, you can ride roughshod over everybody. You think the people of Comfort owe you something, that we have to lick your feet!"

Molly had never thought anything of the kind. But before she could even say so, the voice went on.

"Let me tell you a few things, Miss High-and-Mighty. The McAfees never got anything fair and square. You people never had to work a day or worry like most people in this world. I've kept my eye on your family through the years. I've not been fooled, believe me! Some people in this town still like to see justice. Some people like to see that folks like you don't always have *everything* their own way. There comes a day of reckoning, you know, there *always* comes a day of reckoning!"

"Yes, that's what the Bible says," Molly said. She swallowed hard. Maybe that hadn't been such a good thing to say. What other terrible things could this person think of? Molly should just hang up, perhaps. But the voice would just keep calling.

"Yes, Lord, that's right, a day of reckoning. I'm glad you know the Lord and his ways, at least. Now take your daddy, that smart aleck Mr. Jack — who can stand the sight of him! The good Lord knows that man always had everything he ever wanted handed to him on a silver platter, never had to work a lick in his life!"

"That's not true. My daddy does too work and he works very hard."

The voice snorted. "You McAfees don't know what hard work is, missy! You don't know what most people go through."

"No. You're wrong!"

"No, I am *right*. I have to be. I am on the side of Justice. I *am* the Voice of Truth, and I will not be stilled. I will not be denied. You know that. Your daddy never had to turn his hand, and now he's got what was coming to him! The Lord works in mysterious ways, and even the likes of the McAfees can't escape His stern gaze."

"What do you mean by that?"

"I mean lots of things. I mean your mama, for one. Of course you know that so-called accident on the bridge wasn't any accident at all, but the hand of the Lord coming down to set things right."

"You're wrong. You're wrong and terrible. I don't know who you are, but you're not the Voice of Truth. Everything you say is made up — everything is a lie. I've heard enough."

"No, you haven't, Molly McAfee. You hang up this phone, and you'll be sorry. We are all the Lord's instruments, and we do His earthly bidding. The Lord told me, came to me. Last night I had a vision, Molly McAfee, a visit from the Lord God Himself, and God told me what happened in that mine."

"I don't understand."

"Don't play innocent with me. You know very well what I'm talking about. The mine where my son Albert was killed, Molly McAfee! Your precious mine! The very place where that beast of the field took it into his head to kill my son. The Good Book says man has dominion over the animals, not the other way around. And then you people come to look upon our sorrow and our grief, pretending to want to help. Do you really think you're fooling anyone? 'The serpent wears a false face.' " Now the voice paused. "Ought to have scratched his eyes out, the varmint."

"Now you're talking about my grandfather. You're Mr. Haller's mother! You're not any Voice of Truth."

"Oh, yes. I'm Truth, all right. I've had my vision. The Lord gave it to me to see how that mule up and kicked my only son, my poor baby, and killed him."

"I don't believe you. I don't believe one word of what you say. You don't know *anything* for a fact. How could you say such awful things?" Molly realized how loud her voice had grown; Graham would surely hear her now, come dashing up from the basement, her hands hot and wet and soapy and her apron damp and her hair flying every which way, with a bundle of questions Molly wouldn't know how to answer.

But the voice continued as though it hadn't heard a word of what Molly had said. " . . . and then for them to try to put on all that nicey-nice stuff about your mother. What a joke! I've heard about that camp business and it doesn't impress me one bit. It doesn't *fool* me, either. We all know what you think of us, you high and mighty McAfees. I see you and your mother all the time downtown, Molly McAfee, shopping in your nice clothes, in that big new car of yours."

"What are you talking about? What camp? And my mother is dead. And you don't even *live* in Comfort anymore. You're crazy."

Still the voice continued. " . . . and you McAfees think you can manipulate everything. But I have been given eyes to see all, and I know you have angered the Lord. No matter what they say, Lord, that won't make it right. No. Only the Lord can make things right. And he will, Molly McAfee, he will.

"I have seen the Light," the voice said, growing thin and tired. "I have seen the Truth, and Vengeance is mine, saith the Lord."

"Stop it!" Molly screamed, and she slammed down the phone.

Well, Molly thought, that did it, and she didn't care. Graham must have heard. She would want to know all about who was on the phone, and then she would tell Daddy and Grandpa. But this was none of their worry, this Voice of Truth.

"Exactly what is going on here?" Graham said, rushing into the living room.

"Nothing." Graham would never believe that, but Molly said it.

"Strangest, loudest nothing I ever heard," Graham said. "What was that crash?"

"Oh. That. I dropped the phone," Molly said. On purpose, she thought.

"I guess!" Graham started to go back to her laundry, but then she turned to give Molly a long look. "Are you positive?"

"I'm positive." Graham's look made Molly squirm, so she picked up *Wuthering Heights* again. "Accidents do happen, don't they?"

"Of course, accidents happen." Graham's look turned quizzical. "Molly, you're acting mighty peculiar. Maybe it's not a cold you have — do you have a fever?"

No, not Dr. Tyde, Molly thought. "I'm just fine," she said. "Graham, accidents are just strange, aren't they? I mean how they happen and all, and why — Mama, Mr. Haller — it *was* an accident, wasn't it?"

"It must have been. Until your daddy talks to all the men, and the story gets completely straightened out, we really don't know."

"I know that, about Horace and Mr. Haller. I didn't mean the accident at the mine. I meant Mama's."

12

_◌_ "Grandpa, can't somebody find out how Mr. Haller got hurt?" Molly asked. She was trying to ask casually as she was reading the funnies, and she didn't look up at him.

Grandpa sat in his favorite chair in the whole house, a massive green leather wing chair with diamond-shaped tufts in its back. His long thin arms stretched out on the chair's arms, the newspaper on his lap lay opened to the editorial. But his gold-framed glasses were propped high on his forehead. When Molly looked up to see why he hadn't answered, she could see that Grandpa's eyes were closed. He stirred after a moment, as people will.

"What — what? Did you say something, Molly?"

"I'm sorry, Grandpa. I didn't mean to wake you up."

"It's been such a long day, sweetheart. But it hasn't been an easy one for you, either." Grandpa paused, as if waiting for Molly to say something, but she didn't answer. She glued her eyes back on the funnies. She was never going to find out about Horace.

Grandpa reached up and turned the floor lamp on: one, two clicks. The indirect beam made a golden circle on the study ceiling, spreading warm light out into the room's late afternoon shadows.

"Molly, I know you can remember your mother well."

Molly nodded, but she didn't want to think about it. She didn't want to talk about it. Red Ryder was holed up in a canyon, with only two bullets left.

"And I know your memories are very precious to you. I'm concerned about you."

Alley Oop hit the flying dinosaur on the head. From its beak came stars and spirals and exclamation points.

"Molly?"

"I'm OK."

"Good," Grandpa said. "I want to tell you about something, so you can understand. The Haller family is going to sue the McAfee Coal Company. I feel so sorry for young Mrs. Haller and the children. They'll have to make their case by saying we were at fault. Claiming we had a dangerous mule."

"How do you know?"

"Old Mr. Haller took me aside today, at the cemetery. 'Nothing personal,' he said, and he hoped I could understand. In a way, I can, but not if they have to twist facts. And nobody seems to have the real facts yet."

"So they'll just blame Horace — who can't even defend himself — and you and Daddy."

Grandpa just nodded.

"They can't do that, Grandpa. It's not true — you know that. What makes them so sure it was our fault?"

"Edwards . . . Haller's partner. Each man works with a partner, you know, each pair of men with a mule, and Ike Edwards was Albert Haller's partner. Had been for some time."

"And Ike Edwards says it was Horace's fault?"

"That's what I'm told."

"Whoever said that is a liar. Ike Edwards is a liar, then." Molly closed up the paper, folded it, and put it aside.

"Strong language, Molly."

"I don't care. Edwards is a liar."

"Or he might be mistaken. I haven't heard it from his lips personally."

"Oh, Grandpa! Why do you have to be so nice to everybody? Why should you be nice to people who aren't being nice to you?"

"Molly, it's not over yet. Let's wait and see."

But Molly felt tears burning her eyes, and her face was angry and red. "I know what's going to happen, Grandpa. You're going to have to put Horace to sleep. He doesn't have a chance, does he? Grandpa, if you let that happen, I'll never forgive you."

"Forgive and forget," Mama says. "Come on, Molly, you can't hold a grudge, not on your birth-

day. You're such a big girl now, five years old. You can't stay inside there forever."

Molly is inside the closet, holding her breath. She will stay here forever. Mama doesn't love her enough to give her some of the cake and let her lick the icing bowl.

"Come on, Molly," Mama says. "This cake is for your birthday party. We can't have a big chunk missing out of it when your friends come — how would that look?"

Mama is right.

Molly should come out. The closet is very hot and very stuffy, and it was foolish to come in here and pull the door closed like this. The woolen coat scratches Molly's cheek, and she opens the door just a crack.

Mama's eye looks back in at her.

"Come on, honey, we'll find you something good to eat. I know — I have just the thing! Something you love, something you haven't had in a long, long time, and I have a brand-new box of them. Can you guess what they are?"

"No."

"They come in a special little box, Molly. It looks like a little cage, and it has a handle. Can you guess now?"

"Yes."

"No, you can't. You didn't say. If you know, you have to say."

"I know."

"All right, then, what is it?"

"Crackers. Animal crackers."

* * *

Molly had begged Daddy to let her come with
him and see Horace. Now the big mule stood in
the small separate paddock, where once Daddy
had kept a brood mare with her foal. The foal had
grown up and Daddy had sold them both. Now
it was Horace's isolation cell. Jail. His cage. Molly
peered at the mule through the paddock's high
wooden planks. Horace eyed her back. Was it possible that he understood, with his better-than-
horse sense? Certainly he realized that his routine
had been interrupted. Something was different,
wrong.

If only Horace knew how wrong, Molly thought.

"Come on, Molly," Daddy called, coming out of
the feed barn. Castor, the largest of the orange cats,
trailed behind him. The others — Marilyn and
Putty Paws and Phoebe — watched respectfully
from the barn door. Daddy carried a squat galvan-
ized bucket — almost the size of a small washtub —
heavy with oats, and he had set a bushel basket full
of corn just outside the barn door. "Could you grab
that corn for me?" he asked.

Molly picked up the basket and at Daddy's side
carried it to the mule barn. "You mustn't worry so
about old Horace," Daddy told her. "Things have a
way of turning out. No matter what, you'll learn
something important from all of this."

Molly frowned. "What if I don't like what I
learn?"

"I don't always like what I learn, either, Molly.
But that's the way you put it together."

"Put what together?"

"Being a person, I suppose. Growing up. Not everything will turn out the way we want it."

"I already know that, Daddy."

"Of course," Daddy said. He pushed his lips together hard and pulled his eyebrows down over his eyes.

He must have been thinking of Mama, too.

"Does everything important have to be just the opposite of what we want?"

"Things aren't *that* bad, are they?"

"Right now, I think maybe so."

"No, that's the trick — you have to look at the good with the bad, Molly; that's part of putting it together, too. Nothing's ever all bad, you know, just like nothing's ever all good either. It's how you learn to look at things."

"Maybe people think everything that happens to us McAfees is wonderful and happy, so we deserve to get sued and have people killed every once in a while. I hate Comfort and I hate these mines and I wish I were a million miles away from here."

"No, that wouldn't solve anything, Molly. And no McAfee has ever been a quitter. You'll never convince some people. They've got their minds made up before they start. You have to forget them, and go from there."

Molly and Daddy had reached the mule barn, and Daddy started pouring the long mountain of oats up and down the length of the feed trough.

Outside the closed gate at the other end of the huge barn, the mules watched attentively. Every morning Daddy would see that they were shut out. Otherwise, he told Molly, they'd just hang around in the shade all day and get fat. If he forced them to stay out in the pasture, they'd play their chasing games around the pond and through the willows that bordered the water along the dam.

Molly had to smile. The mules stood like a platoon of soldiers at attention: they waited eagerly while the corn was shucked into the feedbox and the hay flaked and the water run.

Then Daddy spoke. "I hear you've been asking Graham about that secret I never got to tell you, the day of the accident." Daddy rubbed two ears of dry feed corn together. The kernels flew off, dropping mostly into the feedbox.

"Yes."

"Why don't I just tell you about it now. I really meant to before this, but you know how it's been, one thing and then another. I didn't plan for you to be in suspense so long."

Molly took two fresh ears of corn and rubbed them together. "Well, all right."

"OK," Daddy said, taking a deep breath. "You remember the clubhouse on the river? Maybe you don't — it's been a long time since you've been there."

"Oh, sure I remember. We used to go there all the time, with Mama. I wouldn't forget that."

"Yes, well, the surprise is about what Pa and I decided to do with the old place. You know there's quite a lot of woodland out there."

"Is all that woods ours?"

"Yes, pretty much so. Well over five hundred acres. Some beautiful timber out there." Daddy had a faraway look for a minute, but then he took a breath as though he were going to swim a long way underwater.

"Look, Molly, there's a reason we haven't gone back there since your mama died. The clubhouse was an important place to your mama and me. The summer we were married we lived out there all summer — it was our first home. I didn't want to go there and end up thinking about her and just get all sad. That would have been wrong. Does that make sense?"

"Yes, Daddy. But I think about Mama all the time, too."

"I know, Molly. Well, your grandpa and I decided to do something with that clubhouse and the woods that your mother would have liked. Your mother was always trying to help people. And to make a long story short, we had some fixing up and building done — " Daddy stopped. Molly knew. This was the camp that the Voice of Truth had talked about.

Daddy cleared his throat and began again. "I was all set to tell you when this trouble happened. We had planned a big picnic, like a big family reunion, to dedicate the clubhouse as a camp for the miners' children, a place where they can go for a week or so every summer."

"Oh! A camp! Could I go, too?"

"Molly, the camp is for the children who don't have as much as you."

"So it would be wrong for me to go. If it kept someone else from going."

"That's right. But maybe in a year or so you could be a counselor or help in some other way. Does that sound like a good idea?"

"That sounds like a *great* idea."

"I guess I should mention that the camp is going to be named after your mama, Molly. Camp Mary McAfee."

Molly dropped the two bare cobs back into the bushel basket and took the next two. *Camp Mary McAfee.* That sounded wonderful.

"But is it still going to happen?" Molly asked Daddy. "Does Mr. Haller's accident change the plans?"

"It has made things difficult," Daddy answered.

"Because everyone's sad about Mr. Haller, and mad about Horace?"

"Yes," Daddy said, "but mostly because only a few people knew of the plans. Until the accident, none of the miners knew about the camp, but somehow it's on the grapevine now. And I'm afraid it'll look as though the camp is blood money, for Haller's death."

"But that's not the idea at all," Molly said.

"I know it, and you know it. Graham and Lizzie and Pa know it, and the contractor who's done the work out there. But other people might not understand. They had no way of knowing our plans."

"But that's not right, Daddy. Is it your fault if you're trying to do something good and it gets turned against you?"

"I don't know. It's the way it might look that worries me."

"So you won't make it a camp? What about all the work you had done?"

"I don't know what to do yet. Pa and I have to talk it over. Maybe later, maybe after all the questions about Haller's accident are cleared up."

"The camp is for *children*, Daddy. What did children have to do with the accident?" Daddy didn't answer. Then Molly said, "Should I open the gate now?"

"OK. From the bottom," Daddy said.

"From the bottom." Molly ran down the center of the long, open barn. All along the sides, on each of the uprights, were big rings for tying the mules onto, though Daddy never tied them there. He always said they were tied up more than enough down below. They deserved the freedom.

"Watch out, Molly," Daddy called. The mules grew restless as she undid the bottom plank, sliding it through the cleat on the side of the opening. Daddy was flaking the last of the hay. Finally she slid the top plank back, and the dark mules rushed in as if they were coal running out of a chute.

"You'd think they'd never eaten before," Daddy said. "What do you fellows do with the timothy I planted in that pasture?"

Daddy lit a cigarette to think and watch and make sure nobody was picking on anybody at the feed trough.

"Daddy, I want to ask you something about the Mare," Molly said. "It's an idea I got."

"I meant to tell you, Molly, Dr. Tyde called. He says Melissa's still interested in the Mare. For the life of me, I can't figure out why."

Molly didn't have time to worry about Melissa. She had her own plan. "What would you say, Daddy, if I knew how to make the Mare useful? I mean, we wouldn't *have* to sell her then, would we?"

"Oh, Molly, you're so transparent. You mean so that spoiled little Melissa wouldn't get her. That girl needs a good spanking."

"*You* said it, Daddy."

"Well, it depends on what idea you have in mind, Molly. I've told you before it's wrong to let a horse vegetate like that, and I stand by what I said. I just won't have it. It's cruel. They die young, you know, if they don't work."

"The Mare won't vegetate."

"All right then. What do you have in mind?"

"Well, I got this idea the other day. I mean, I was just saddle-soaping her tack, and there it was — right on the tin: 'Harnesses,' it said.

"I know. So?"

"I want to teach the Mare to drive."

"You mean pull a cart?"

"Yes. I know I can teach her. I can teach her anything."

"But Molly, she's a saddle horse. Pony, I mean. And you don't have a cart. You don't have harnesses. You have to realize you'd be starting from scratch."

"I'll find harnesses. I'll go to the fairgrounds and find out all about it from Mr. Steward, the man with the hackneys, and he can help me find some used gear, and maybe I'll even be able to borrow a little sulky to start with."

"Whoa, Molly! You do sound as though you have it all planned, I have to admit. But do you realize how hard it will be getting the Mare used to pulling something? It won't happen overnight, you know."

"I know, Daddy. But I did teach her to jump. She couldn't do that before either."

"That's true. So you've made up your mind, have you?"

"Please, Daddy. I want to keep the Mare. Forever."

"I don't know what to say. You are something, Molly. I'll give you credit. It never would have occurred to me." Daddy stubbed out his cigarette and sloshed water from the trough to make sure it was out.

"Please, Daddy, please promise not to sell the Mare until I try. You won't be sorry."

Daddy didn't say anything. He squashed the cigarette and it came apart.

"Melissa wouldn't be nice to her, you know," Molly added.

"I know. She's got a mean streak in her, that girl." Daddy looked at Molly and finally said, "All right, Molly, you can give it a try."

"And we're going to dedicate the camp for Mama, too, aren't we?"

"You drive a hard bargain, daughter," Daddy said, giving her a big hug and a kiss. "We'll talk to Pa."

When they reached Horace's paddock, the big mule came slowly over to the fence. Daddy gave him his ration of oats with the vitamin drops, and corn, and Molly held a flake of hay out to him. But Horace stood quietly, his head even with his withers. He snuffled but didn't take any hay. He didn't move toward his feedbox, either, though Daddy rattled the corn and encouraged him gently to come and eat.

Was something wrong with Horace?

Why wasn't he acting like the regular old Horace, the one they could always depend on?

Horace, not Ducat, wears Mama's flat English saddle. Horace is also tacked with the four-rein bridle with the snaffle bit and no browband.

Molly looks up at him. It has been a difficult trial, but Horace is up to the challenge. There is no obstacle too high or wide or difficult for Horace. His time in the cross-country is the best of the field, and yesterday he outscored everyone with his performance in dressage. Today is stadium jumping.

The crowd murmurs incredulously as Molly McAfee's name is called with Horace the mule as her mount.

"Ha, ha, ha!" says Melissa in her tennis whites.

"Ha, ha! Ha, ha!" say Mrs. Tyde and Dr. Tyde, punching each other in the ribs.

*"Are you sure you know what you're doing?"
Daddy says, giving Molly a leg up.*

*"This had better be good!" the Voice of Truth
says from a small gray rain cloud stuck in the
branches of a chestnut tree.*

"Shut up! She's my best friend," Luke says.

*Horace looks around at Molly. It is the same
look he gave her the day she first rode him. Horace
says nothing in regular language, but in a look he
says: I am the same Horace. Believe in me.*

And Molly does.

13

"Land sakes, Pa," Lizzie said. "You've done so much work on this place! I can't get over how wonderful it looks."

And the old clubhouse really did shine in its glistening white paint. On one side of the cottage, an addition as big as the original building had been built on, making two new bunk rooms. The old porch, which also served as a dining room, was doubled in size too, and now had windows that could be closed in case of bad weather. Two long tables, each with a dozen chairs, were covered with huge red-and-white-checked tablecloths, just like the ones that Mama had always kept on the clubhouse table. In the kitchen was an immense new stove with all sorts of giant pots and pans from Comfort Restaurant Supply. Everything was shining and new. And outside, at the edge of the clearing, two tent platforms had been built for older campers. There, big new green tents stood with their flaps tied open to welcome visitors.

Five weeks had passed since Mr. Haller died — five weeks that sometimes seemed the longest weeks Molly had ever known. Mrs. Haller, Sr., had disappeared, and people were saying the shock had been too much for her and that she went back to Arkansas. She was better off there, people said, with her daughter. But nothing was settled about the accident. Things were quiet — too quiet to suit Molly. Daddy and Grandpa decided to go ahead with the camp dedication, and said they just hoped everyone would understand how long the plans had been in the making — since long before Mr. Haller's accident.

June had turned to July. Melissa Tyde was still in town. She had called twice when Molly was out working with the Mare and the harness, Graham said, but didn't leave a message. Finally, the third time, Molly felt she had to face Melissa and called her back.

"Melissa," Molly said, "if you really want to come and ride the pony again, it'd be all right with me."

"Oh?" Melissa said. She sounded surprised, as if she expected to have to argue with Molly, or plead. It had been too easy. "Well, when?"

"Anytime," Molly said, thinking this must be what Graham meant when she told Molly to kill Melissa with kindness. It seemed to be working. "The Mare's always here, and so am I. If you give me fifteen minutes' warning, I'll have her tacked and ready to go."

"Well," Melissa said, sounding very dubious, "I'll

have to check with my daddy and see when he can bring me."

"All right," Molly said. "Really, any time is fine. OK," she added, thinking that was the end, "'bye."

"Wait, Molly, to tell you the truth . . . " Melissa hesitated. "I'm not sure, actually, that your pony is the right one for me."

"You mean because of . . . what happened when you rode her before?"

"Oh, no! Not at all," said the same old Melissa. "*Daddy* says that's all the more reason to ride her. Daddy knows so much about horses. More than we'll ever know." She paused, and her voice changed. "Daddy said I had to call you."

Molly said nothing.

"The thing is, maybe I'd better wait, Molly. Don't you think so? I mean until after I get some more experience, at camp? It's all right with you, isn't it? I promised Daddy I'd talk to you."

"Sure, Melissa," Molly said.

"Oh!" Melissa said. "I just remembered! I've got to run, Molly. I'm late for my tennis lesson at the club. See you, Molly."

And then, instead of hating Melissa, Molly suddenly felt very sorry for her. What a complicated life Melissa must have — those parents, all that scooting about. Molly wanted to tell her not to worry, and all about the driving, but Melissa had hung up.

Officially Molly hadn't told anyone what she was up to with the Mare other than Mr. Steward, who had a pair of prize hackney ponies at the fairgrounds stable. Mr. Steward reminded Molly of Grandpa, and right off he told her to call him "Stew." Stew brought Molly one of his old harnesses, too small for his animals, he claimed. "If you get some use out of this," he said, "that'll be payment enough." The new get-up took a lot of explaining to the Mare, but finally she understood. It was this or else. Molly didn't have any kind of cart for the Mare to pull; for now the harnesses were enough of a challenge, and Molly ran alongside as she taught her to go through her gaits.

But, the dedication picnic would be a challenge of another kind.

It was a hot afternoon toward the end of July. The trees barely moved and the birds were silent in the heat. The smooth tan river, at the foot of the long hill in front of the house, moved slowly, without a sound. Two o'clock finally came.

The miners with their families arrived in clutches. The men were dressed for the special oc- casion — suits and ties, with pale straw summer hats for some. Their wives wore good summer dresses and high-heeled shoes, hats with veils, and white cotton gloves. The children looked ready for Sunday school: girls' hair in neat braids, boys' slicked down, combed into wet-looking teeth that still stood separated. The children were behaving; they were almost too quiet and too mannerly to be having a good time.

"Come on, men," Daddy said, pumping the handle on the top of the silvery keg, "help yourself to a brew. George . . . Phil . . . now don't be shy. Come on, lead the way." Two men came to the keg. "I'll pump for a while, Jack," one of them said.

"Soda for the kids is in those tubs over there," Daddy said. "Molly, Luke, lend a hand with the bottle openers," and he nodded toward washtubs heaped with ice and soda bottles of every color. The men clustered around the keg, filling their beer glasses faster than Molly could say "lickety-split." The ladies drew into talkative knots under two pecan trees, and Grandpa went from one group to the next to say hello to everyone. It seemed people would never stop coming!

Luke said, "I'm having a root beer," as Molly knew he would — Luke believed that root beer sounded grown up. He popped off the cap and caught the foam just as it was about to spill out. Most of the kids had their sodas now, and Molly wanted to think. She walked to the edge of the field Grandpa had mown for parking. Cars were still coming, but slowly now.

"I'm Molly McAfee," she said to the next carload of people. "I'm glad you came today." That seemed to make people smile and feel at home, and she said it to the next two cars that came. Then a funny old maroon car, a Plymouth, she thought, chugged uncertainly down the dirt road, a cloud of dust growing in its wake. Maybe this was the last car, Molly thought, and then she saw who was in it. The Hallers. What would she say to them?

"Molly McAfee, please come here," Miss Curran says.

Molly is coloring. Can't Miss Curran see that? Molly is busy, doing important things here. She is right in the middle of the biggest and best rainbow ever colored at Longfellow School. She has already finished with her seatwork. Are her shoes not tied? What is wrong with Miss Curran, anyway? Miss Curran always says you should finish what you start, and now she's not letting Molly finish this.

Molly looks up and Miss Curran looks terrible. Not scary or mean, the way lots of kids claim she looks, but just terrible. Something is all wrong with her face, but Molly can't figure out what it is. She's never seen Miss Curran look this way, and she's been in her class for almost a whole year now. Molly starts to put the crayons away.

"That's all right, dear," Miss Curran says. "I'll do it."

What? Miss Curran put somebody's crayons away? Something really is wrong here. Miss Curran has a rule: everyone must put away his own materials. That is the most important rule in first grade. Materials—that means everything. But especially things like crayons.

"Molly, just please come here, dear," Miss Curran says.

Dear? What is this "dear"? Miss Curran is the strictest teacher at Longfellow. She doesn't call anybody "dear," and she's just called Molly that twice.

Molly looks up again and sees Miss Curran looking desperately out the door into the hall. Molly's eyes follow Miss Curran's, and there in the hall she sees a blue-uniformed policeman, with his hat in his hand, and Daddy, crying.

Grandpa pulled his gold watch out of his pocket, like someone pulling in a fish. He popped open the watch and peered at it through the bottom of his bifocals. "Three o'clock, son," he said to Daddy. "It's time."

Molly looked across the faces in the crowd. There were so many people. Molly didn't know them, but they all knew who she was.

Elaine kept her head down, avoiding Molly's eyes. Old Mr. Haller, Elaine's grandfather, was here, which surprised Molly. He stood next to Elaine's mother. Molly felt something boiling inside her, her heart beating fast. What was *he* doing here — this Mr. Haller who didn't want the lawsuit to be anything personal. Elaine stood with each hand on a younger brother's shoulder, talking to them, not looking up or around at all.

"Friends," Grandpa began, "some of you know that Jack and I had been looking forward to this day since last winter. Last New Year's Day we sat talking about resolutions and what we wanted to accomplish during the coming year, and today was one of the things we decided on."

"We wanted this to be a happy occasion for all of our families, but today's happiness is tempered by our loss of Albert Haller. Before we begin, let's together observe a moment of silence in Albert's memory and resolve to stand behind Martha Haller and her family."

Grandpa paused. The afternoon was completely still.

Leaves.

River.

Air.

Insects.

Nothing moved, nothing made a sound.

Then Grandpa cleared his throat. Molly looked up and saw Elaine's mother blow her nose and look away, toward the woods. "Now you can take over, Jack," Grandpa said.

"I'm not really one for making speeches," Daddy began, taking some folded papers out of his pocket. He looked at them for a long moment, then put them away. "I just can't read the speech I wrote," he said. His voice had a funny crack in it. "If you don't mind, I'll just talk to you the way I do every day.

"My wife Mary loved people, and children in particular. I know she would be very happy to see children enjoying this place again, as those in our family did." Daddy cleared his throat and took a deep breath. "So, I dedicate this land as Camp Mary McAfee, in the hope that her spirit will live on here, and that our children will have only glad times in this place."

Molly felt a tear slip out of her left eye, then another out of the right. Why didn't she have a hankie? What would Mama say?

*Elaine Haller has on a mink coat, full length,
three thick diamond bracelets, and she waves a
huge lace handkerchief. Her hair is suddenly beautiful and very blond, and she looks like something
out of a Ponds Cold Cream ad, merely one of the
world's Ten Most Beautiful Women.* "Hello, Molly,
darling," *she says.* "Are you still paring horses'
hooves and mucking out those gross stables?"

"Well, yes," *says Molly, mystified.*

"I'm not, love," *says Elaine, gesturing with her
impeccably manicured long nails.* "I haven't the
time for that, not with all the travel. You should
have seen *the winter collections in Paris, Molly,
dear. They were simply* de trop — *too much, you
know. Ah, no, I suppose you don't know, do you,
poor darling? The McAfees aren't up to travel or
French or much else these days, are they?"*

"What's wrong with you, Elaine?"

"Nothing, darling, I *couldn't be better. Life is
wonderful, after all. Everybody should have a
daddy like mine!"*

"You're terrible, making puns. Shameless. Disgusting. And certainly not funny!"

"Au contraire, chérie," *Elaine says.* "That's what
you think."

"I *don't know what to think anymore," Molly
says, and her hands grow cold as ice, and the cold
spreads up her arms and toward her heart.*

Luke stood there, grinning like a perfect fool.

"Told you it was cold," he said. "There aren't

any more root beers. You'll have to have orange or R-C Cola. Hey, Eddie, want to play catch?" Luke darted off with a classmate he found in the crowd.

"Molly looks a thousand miles away from here," Lizzie said, giving her a hug from behind.

"I kind of am," Molly said. Molly saw Elaine Haller, still herding two little brothers. She didn't have on any diamond bracelets or look as though she'd been anywhere near Paris. She wore the same pale blue too-big dress that she had on that night that Billy and Karl dug under the wiegelas.

"Have you spoken to Elaine?" Lizzie asked. "You really should, you know." But Molly felt awkward. There was no easy way just to go up to Elaine, exactly, since they hadn't talked since that strange night before the funeral. So much had happened since. The closeness they had felt then seemed so far away.

Besides, Molly had some questions. What, Molly wondered, did Elaine know about her grandmother pretending to be the Voice of Truth? Did she know about the lawsuit? Or did Elaine know all those things and feel just as awkward as Molly? Elaine might just hate her.

Throw your heart over the fence and jump after it, Molly, the jumping coach always said. Molly didn't think she and the Mare could take the coop, but they did. And they had to try, to do it.

"Hi, Elaine." Molly's voice came out tight and small.

"Hi, Molly. How are you?"

"I'm fine, Elaine. Are you OK?"

"Yes. This is a nice picnic, Molly. And the camp will be a wonderful place for Billy and Karl to come."

"There'll be a lot of great things to do around here. You should come, too."

"Well, no."

"Why not? Don't you want to?"

Elaine tilted her head forward, hiding her eyes. "I'd love to come to camp here. I just can't."

"Why?"

"My mother . . . "

"You mean she won't let you come?"

"It's not that. She needs me. Mom has a job now, and I have to take care of the little ones. Soon the baby, too. I won't have time to go to camp."

"Oh," Molly said.

Of course — how stupid of her. Molly should have thought, she should have realized. What could she say now that wouldn't make things even worse?

But "Excuse me, Elaine," was all Molly could manage. She felt a lump in her throat growing bigger by the second, and it looked as though Elaine was going to cry.

Molly went inside the clubhouse and sat down at one of the long tables and cried, too. Nothing made any sense, absolutely nothing. Elaine couldn't do things other kids could, and she hadn't done anything to deserve to be punished; Horace was being blamed for something she *knew* he didn't do. Mama on the bridge hadn't done anything wrong. Large, hot tears rolled down her cheeks in steady streams.

Molly wishes all motorcycles to be instantly and forever nowhere, banished, condemned.

Molly wishes such things as motorcycles didn't exist and never had. Molly wishes that Mama's beautiful, shining, whole new car hadn't met the stranger's motorcycle on the bridge over the Mississippi and hadn't swerved to miss it and then hit the rail and gone through.

Molly wishes the terrible dreams would stop, nightmares of metal tearing metal, dreams of Mama in the air, falling, falling, the way people always do in nightmares, never getting to the bottom. But what happened to Mama wasn't a dream. Mama had gotten to the bottom. Mama's car had hit the water, the brown, angry Mississippi swirling with the spring flood, and she couldn't even get out of the car to swim. The motorcycle driver ran head on into an oncoming truck and was killed instantly.

It served him right, Molly thinks. It is wrong, she knows, to think such a terrible thing.

But Mama hadn't done anything wrong. She was only trying not to hit the crazy man on the motorcycle. What was wrong with him, driving like that on that bridge? Why had he made Mama have the wreck? It was his fault. Why did Mama have to pay? Why did he do it? Why did it have to happen at all? "Some things we never understand," *Grandpa told her.* "Some things are just mysteries. We just

*have to decide which those are, and let them go,
Molly.*"

Molly wanted to go home.

Where was Daddy? Maybe Graham could drive
her. Daddy wouldn't be able to leave. Molly
scanned the crowd. There he was, off at the edge of
the crowd, talking earnestly to one of the men.

Then Daddy also began to look around, as though
he too were looking for someone. Still talking and
looking around, Daddy and the man walked toward
the clubhouse. When he looked at the porch door,
Daddy found what he was looking for.

"There you are, Molly! I've been looking all over
for you."

Molly wiped her eyes with the back of her hand
as the two men came in and sat down at the table
with her.

"Molly, this is Ike Edwards," Daddy said. "My
daughter, Molly."

The man's rough hand took Molly's and shook it
hard. Molly felt sick, like in the car, like with flowers. Terrible, awful Ike Edwards. The man who
told lies about Horace. Molly couldn't see why
Daddy was introducing him to her. She could do
without, thank you.

"Pleased to meet you," Ike Edwards said with a
shy smile.

"Molly, Ike came to me this afternoon to tell me
something. You remember, he was the man working
with Albert Haller the day of the accident."

"Yes, I remember. You told me." Molly saw no reason to smile at this man.

"Well, Molly, you were right about Horace. Would you mind repeating what you just told me, Ike? She's been defending that mule since the very beginning."

"Well, Mr. Jack, like Martha Haller says, right is right. And it's wrong, making two mistakes out of one."

Molly looked at Ike Edwards. What was he talking about? She studied the hard, lean man, scrubbed white and serious in his suit and tie. His smile was gone now.

"Ike's been telling me about the accident, Molly. You had the right idea."

"You mean Horace didn't hurt Mr. Haller?"

"No, Horace wouldn't hurt a fly," Ike Edwards answered. "Best mule ever pulled a cart." He cleared his throat. "I haven't slept a sound night since Bert's accident."

Molly frowned. What had he told Daddy? What was he trying to say? "I don't understand," she said.

"We all thought it would somehow help," Ike Edwards said, "if we agreed on some story."

"A *story?*" Molly said. "You mean you made something up? About Horace?"

"Please — you don't understand — that wasn't the idea. Bert was my best friend — I thought he was already dead. Everyone just went along — everyone said ... " His words trailed off as he looked at Daddy.

"Like I said, Jack, I keep seeing it, over and over. In my sleep, all day, every day. I had to tell Martha how it really was. I see it again and again, a million times, but I still can't figure it. I never will understand."

"Mr. Edwards," Molly said, "what *did* happen?"

"That's just it. I don't know how the cave-in could have happened, but I can tell you Horace had nothing to do with it. Nowhere near. Just one minute me and Bert were working, like always — Bert was whistling, I remember. Always was a willing worker, Bert. Always whistled." Ike Edwards' chin puckered. He bit his lip.

"Ike went to Mrs. Haller, Molly, and told her all this."

"I just couldn't keep it inside me. I told her it wasn't Bert who blamed the mule, because one minute Bert was whistling and working, and the next — Bert didn't say anything. He was unconscious from the second the cave-in happened. And Martha had a right to know Bert wasn't in any pain."

"But you blamed Horace," Molly said.

"I know it was wrong. I never felt right about it, but I didn't know what else to do. I listened to what everybody else said, not to what I knew. The men only thought they were doing right by Martha and the kids. But when I told her what really happened, she wouldn't hear of leaving things as they were. 'Either you're going to tell the McAfees,' she said, 'or I'm going to. Maybe I'm a fool,' she said to me, 'but I'd never sleep a sound night either, knowing this.'

"So that's the story, and the truth. Martha Haller's one fine woman, drawing the line like that. Not many like her."

14

ᔐ "Is the table all set, Molly? Graham calls from the kitchen. "Remember, eight places. Oh, it's going to be so wonderful having a party again — it's been such a long time!"

Again Molly is inside her lattice porch.
It is the end of summer, some summer.
Which summer is it?
Molly pulls herself toward the lathes. She touches the morning-glory's leaves. She breathes the end of August, hears crickets and locusts singing, clicking on in time.

The sun dapples the inside of the lattice porch. Graham is actually singing in the kitchen, so full of the plans for Molly's birthday party, which she *almost* kept a secret. Molly says she might as well help Graham as long as she knows about the party. But for some strange reason, Molly almost feels that it is Graham who is helping her.

Dinner will be in the dining room tonight, Molly's birthday dinner. A family party: Lizzie and Ned — back in town for the next two days — and Luke and Daddy and Grandpa and Graham and Molly. The table needs two extra leaves.

And there is one extra guest. Elaine, because she and Molly started talking again that afternoon at the camp, and since that day have talked many times. Molly knows Elaine must be a real friend because they can talk and talk and never run out of things to say.

Molly thinks about the long summer. It started right here on the porch, with her thinking about how the summer would take forever.

September first. Can the summer have flown so fast? Is it really gone already? In a way it seems the summer has lasted a lifetime, but in another it was over in an instant. So much has happened.

This summer is over. Molly is twelve.

Mama sits on the edge of the bed in her quiet room. She is dressed to go out. Molly wonders where.

"Hello, lamb," she says softly to Molly.

Molly comes through the door, into Mama's room. Mama looks a little different too.

"Where are you going, Mama?"

"I have to go away, Molly. A kind of trip."

"Where?"

"That's not important, lamb," Mama says. "Molly, let me look at you. I hardly know you, you've grown so."

"It's these legs. They've made me too tall for the Mare."

"That's all right, honey. Having long legs is not the end of the world. It's part of growing up."

"I'm teaching her how to drive — to pull a cart, Mama."

"I know, darling, it's wonderful! You see, you needn't have worried about things so — everything is turning out all right. I'm sure of it now."

"I hope so."

"Oh, it will. Now that's a beautiful white dress you have on. Did you and Lizzie find it at Gold's?"

"Yes. You knew that, didn't you?"

"Yes."

"It was the dress for the camp dedication. You know about that, too, don't you?"

"Yes. I'm glad you picked that dress, Molly. It suits you perfectly."

"I picked it because you would like it, Mama."

"That's sweet, Molly, but I hope you will do things because you want to, not because you think they'll please someone else. First you have to make yourself happy, sweetheart."

Tiptoeing slowly so all twelve candles will stay lit, Graham brings Molly's chocolate birthday cake in from the kitchen. Everyone at the table turns and says "Ah!" and sings "Happy Birthday." Graham puts the huge chocolate cake down in front of Molly.

Molly closes her eyes and makes her birthday

wish — a wish she can never tell anybody. Molly thinks of other birthdays: the one when she hid in the closet, the one when the Mare came to live with her. She thinks how Melissa Tyde almost took the Mare away — and how foolish those fears look now. Poor Melissa. Molly had invited her to the birthday party, but Melissa had the Labor Day Tennis Tournament at the Comfort Country Club. "Mama's making me," Melissa said. "And I'm allergic to horses, Molly," she said. "I got asthma at camp from them." And Molly thinks of this birthday morning, and Daddy's wide smile when he said "Happy Birthday, Molly — look outside," and the little red cart was parked under the elms next to the pump Grandpa and Luke painted together, so long ago. In an instant Molly remembers a million things: Daddy saying that everything would turn out all right. Grandpa saying not to worry about what you couldn't help. About not giving up on the things that really meant something to you.

Molly opens her eyes and sees the candles, their tiny flames flickering, and all the faces, waiting, smiling.

She takes a deep breath. And she blows out every one of the candles.

Molly knows that wishes do come true.

"Everything is going to be all right, Mama. You don't need to worry about me or anything while you're on your trip."

"I can see that, Molly."

"*I will be able to take care of things.*"

"*Yes, I think you can, Molly. Now, I think you can.*"

"*School will be starting again soon, Mama. I'll be in seventh grade.*"

"*Oh, so soon! Just yesterday you were going off to kindergarten, it seems — your very first day. You must use your mind, Molly, always. Promise me.*"

"*I promise, Mama.*"

"*It's very important. You mustn't be afraid to think.*"

"*I'm not, Mama.*"

"*I know, sweetheart. I can tell. And Molly, always look for the good in people.*"

"*I do, I will.*"

"*I know.*"

"*Mama, do you really have to go?*"

"*It isn't for me to decide, Molly. Time changes things.*"

"*But why have you packed up everything like this? Mama, won't you please leave some of your things here? It makes me sad, it looks as though you're not ever coming back if you take everything with you.*"

"*They're only things I won't need anyway, Molly. You don't want them around here, cluttering things up.*"

"*They won't clutter things up, Mama. I'm glad they're here. They're yours and they remind me of you.*"

"*Molly.*" Mama's smile is gone.

"What, Mama?"

"You won't need things *to remind you of me."*

Molly looks around Mama's room. The closet door is open and all of Mama's pretty clothes are gone, and there is nothing there but a great many empty hangers. The dresser, too, is cleared, and Molly knows the drawers are all empty. Even the dressing table is bare, except for the picture of Mama, taken years ago, in its oval silver frame. All of Mama's French perfume is gone, and her silver comb and brush and mirror. Everything looks so bare, so empty, but somehow the room isn't exactly empty. There is still something of Mama here, something Molly can't put into words, to touch or tell the color of. Even the picture on the dressing table doesn't exactly matter, Molly thinks.

"No, Mama," Molly says, "you're right. I won't need things."

"So, then," Mama says, closing her purse and putting it on her knees, "I'd better be going."

"You really won't be coming back, will you?" Molly holds her lower lip tight between her teeth to keep it still.

"Molly, it's not a question of going or staying," Mama says. "It depends on how you look at it. In one way, I'm not going anywhere, you know — I'm staying right here. But in another way, Molly, I am going. The way I am, the way you are — in that way, I am going, because you don't need me anymore. It's not so awful, really. Don't look so glum. Look at the bright side."

"What bright side?"

"Now you know what I mean. You're practically grown up. And, Molly, I'm so proud of you."

Molly's lip gets loose and shakes. Tears come rushing down her cheeks, but more tears are forming inside — her face and head feel like one gigantic tear. Molly sniffs, loudly.

"Here, lamb," Mama says, "take my hankie."

Molly sniffs again. "It's all right, Mama," Molly says, reaching into her pocket. "I have one of my own."

Mama smiles a smile that lasts forever.

And then Mama is gone.